Rez Runaway

Rez Runaway

Melanie Florence

James Lorimer & Company Ltd., Publishers
Toronto

James Lorimer & Company Ltd., Publishers acknowledges the support of the
Ontario Arts Council (OAC), an agency of the Government of Ontario, which
in 2015-16 funded 1,676 individual artists and 1,125 organizations in 209 com-
munities across Ontario for a total of $50.5 million. We acknowledge the support
of the Canada Council for the Arts, which last year invested $153 million to bring
the arts to Canadians throughout the country. This project has been made possible in part by the Government of Canada and with the support of the Ontario
Media Development Corporation.

Cover design: Tyler Cleroux
Cover image: Shutterstock

978-1-4594-1165-4
eBook also available 978-1-4594-1163-0

Cataloguing data available from Library and Archives Canada.

Published by:
James Lorimer & Company Ltd.,
Publishers
117 Peter Street, Suite 304
Toronto, ON, Canada
M5V 0M3
www.lorimer.ca

Distributed by:
Lerner Publishing Services
1251 Washington Ave N
Minneapolis, MN, USA
55401
www.lernerbooks.com

Printed and bound in Canada.
Manufactured by Friesens Corporation in Altona, Manitoba, Canada in
December 2016.
Job #228980

For my family — Chris, Josh, and Taylor. You make my life an adventure.

Prologue

My name is Joe Littlechief and I grew up knowing that there was something different about me.

I lived in a place where the smell of fry bread was always in the air. We hunted for food rather than for sport. Our reserve didn't have a casino or anything. We lived pretty simply. But it was home and I didn't know any other life.

For the most part, I guess I was a typical seventeen-year-old. I played soccer with my friends. We gathered on Friday nights to talk and dance and just hang out. I had an old beater that I bought for fifty bucks from Harry Lafontaine, but it didn't run most of the time. I tinkered with the car when I had the time. I watched hockey and played PS4.

Like a lot of kids on the rez, I lived with just my mom. It's not like I had any pent up feelings about my parents' divorce. It had happened when I was so young that all I ever knew was having only my mom to rely on. No need for a therapist or anything. Mom loved church. Something to do with her years with the nuns I guess. I never could figure out why my grandfather sent her and my aunt to a residential school. He had spent most of his childhood in one being abused. But my mom had a better experience and the one thing she took away from the school was a deep faith in God. She was pretty devout. She took the whole commandment thing pretty seriously and the priest's word was law. The church community set the standard for her life, and she really relied on it when she and my dad split up. From what she told me, Dad had been a sporadic churchgoer and much less strict with the rules. Maybe that's why their marriage didn't work.

My friends and I have as much fun as we can find on the rez. As a group, we hang out in a clearing in the woods, talking shit, and flirting with the girls. Sometimes someone would grab a bottle out of their parents' stash and we'd pass it around. Truthfully, I'd usually fake it. I'd bring it to my lips and pretend to take a drink. I got good at grimacing and choking in what I assumed was the usual reaction to the rum or rye or whatever they'd taken.

My father had been a drinker. I didn't remember much about him but I remembered that. Stumbling into the house in the middle of the night, stinking of booze and smoke. Groping at my mom. Sometimes taking a swing at her. She'd beg him to repent — to come to church and renounce Satan and the evils of drink. He'd refuse and drink harder. My mom finally kicked him out and he left to start a family with someone who shared his love of the local watering hole. I haven't seen him since. No big loss. Like I said, I didn't remember any good times with my dad. And I knew I didn't want to end up like him.

See, for the most part I'm just a normal, average teenaged boy. Except for one thing. When all the guys sat around and talked about the girls they wanted to hook up with or commented on how big Maggie Running Wolf's boobs were getting, I found myself looking at Benjy — a kid I had known since we were babies. I'd look at my best friend talking about Maggie and I'd wonder what it would feel like to kiss him instead.

Chapter 1

Aunt Ava

I usually spent Saturday mornings with my mom, drinking coffee and catching up. My mom filled me in on her visits with my Aunt Ava and what she learned at church or bible study or women's group. She talked about what she was planting in her garden and what she was going to cook over the next week. I mostly talked about school. She loved to hear about what I was learning or reading. I showed her what I was working on in my sketchbook.

She was one of the few people who knew how much I loved to draw. I told her about the funny things Benjy said or the huge fish I caught but threw back. It was something we had done together since I was a kid, except for me drinking coffee.

"So I saw the way that Betsy's granddaughter was looking at you at Paulette's fish fry," my mom said slyly. She peered at me over the rim of her steaming mug.

I blew on my own coffee and avoided her eyes. "Roz. Yeah. I know."

"She's a nice girl, that Roz."

Oh she's shrewd, I thought. Like any mom, she was curious about my love life, which was pretty much non-existent. Rather than being relieved that I wasn't out running around with a bunch of girls, she worried about it. She asked a million questions. *Why aren't you dating anyone? Why are you so picky? What's wrong with Betsy's granddaughter?* She was now in full on matchmaker mode.

"Yeah. She's really nice," I said simply.

"And so pretty."

"Sure," I mumbled.

"So?" she prompted.

"So what?" I asked. I was acting dumb, even though I knew that drove my mom crazy.

She raised an eyebrow at me. "So . . . you should ask her out after church. She could come over for lunch."

"Mom!" I felt my face burning. There was a fine line between a casual interest in my dating life and actually pimping me out to her friend's granddaughter.

"What? You're seventeen. You should go out once in a while with a nice girl."

"I do go out, Mom," I grumbled. I took a huge gulp of coffee and nearly spit it across the table at her when the lava-hot liquid seared my tongue.

"With your friends," she pointed out.

"You like my friends."

"I do," she admitted. "But some of them

never set foot inside the church. And some of them go out more than I think is proper."

"But I don't go out enough?" I asked, teasing her.

She shrugged. "I just worry that growing up without your father around maybe didn't give you much of an example on how to have a relationship."

I smiled at her. "Mom, I promise you that you haven't damaged me or anything. If I meet someone I like enough to ask out, I will. Okay?"

"Okay." She smiled back. "Are you coming to church with me tomorrow?"

"Yeah, maybe. Depends what time I get in, I guess." I smirked at her. "See? I go out."

"Yeah, yeah." She stood up and shuffled over to the refrigerator and started pulling out eggs and bacon to make some breakfast.

"I'll help," I told her, standing up and taking the egg carton from her.

"Anyone home?" My Aunt Ava breezed

through the back door and sauntered into the kitchen. It was her usual greeting, even though everyone on the rez knew when my mom was in. My mom and her sister had a standing date on Saturdays to cook and gossip. Aunt Ava lived with my grandfather in the tiny house the sisters had grown up in. I suspected that their Saturday mornings were more about her getting away from him than from a need to catch up on who was fighting with who on the rez.

Aunt Ava set a bag of vegetables from my grandfather's garden, a loaf of her fresh-baked bread, and one of her world-famous apple pies on the counter. She leaned down to kiss me on the cheek before pouring herself a cup of coffee and flopping into the chair across from me.

"Did you tell him we saw Betsy's granddaughter at Paulette's fish fry?" Aunt Ava asked my mom. She took a sip of her coffee before dumping several spoonfuls of sugar into it and stirring it idly.

I rolled my eyes.

"I did," my mother replied.

"And?"

My mother shrugged.

"I'm sitting right here," I waved at them.

Aunt Ava turned to look at me. "So, smart guy? What do you think of her? What's her name? Ron?"

Ron? "Roz," I corrected her. "She's nice. Not really my type though." *That was an understatement*, I thought.

"Oh really? And what is your type?" she asked.

My mother smiled. She loved when her sister came over and backed her up.

"My type?" I stalled. *Batman. Superman. Pretty much any hot superhero in a skin-tight suit.* "I don't know. Maybe that girl from that show? I forget her name." *Smooth, Joe,* I mocked myself. I was practically sweating. It was one thing to get around my mom's questions. But it was a lot harder when there were two of them ganging up on me.

My aunt cocked her head at me, her eyebrows raised. "Which girl? From which show?"

"The girl!" I said, not meeting her eyes. "You know!"

But I saw the look that passed between my aunt and my mom. It was time for me to beat a hasty retreat before I was buried under a landslide of questions.

I hated lying to them. Especially to my mother. It had just been the two of us for so long. It didn't feel right to be dishonest. But if I *was* being honest, I was afraid of what my mom would think. What would she do if she knew that it wasn't some big-breasted, empty-headed starlet I lusted after? She was the person I loved and trusted the most in the world. And I was afraid to tell her that the celebrities I dreamed about were usually much less . . . feminine.

I swallowed and ducked my head, taking one last gulp of coffee. I swallowed my truth down with it.

I kissed each of them on the cheek.

"You need someone more exciting to gossip about," I told them.

Aunt Ava laughed and cut a thick slice of still-warm bread from the loaf she had baked that morning. She slathered it with my mom's homemade strawberry jam and handed it to me.

"Off with you," she winked. She turned toward my mom. "Did you hear about what happened to the Thibideaus?" Clearly I was no longer the hot topic.

My mother nodded at Aunt Ava. But there was something about the way her eyes lingered on me as I strode out the door. Had she guessed more about me than she was willing to admit?

Chapter 2

Secrets

It's not easy having a secret. It's even harder trying to keep one on the rez. Everyone knows everyone else's business. Say you found out that your man was cheating on you and wanted to cry on your kokum's shoulder. Your grandmother would already know all about it by the time you walked across the rez to her house.

Let me give you another example. I hadn't really dated much, for obvious reasons I suppose. But my friends started planning this group date, which was really just a bunch of us hanging out in our usual clearing in the woods. I figured the easiest thing to do was just go along with it. No matter what we called them, these parties or dates or whatever didn't entail much more than sitting around the fire and talking about sports or school. Once in a while, someone would take a date farther into the woods for some privacy.

Let's face it. I didn't want to go on a date, group or otherwise. I wanted to head out with Benjy and Marcus and Marcus's younger brother, Draco. (Their mother was a big Harry Potter fan . . . although why she named her kid after the biggest jerk in the movie and not the hero is anyone's guess.) I wanted to meet up with the other guys and not have to worry about fending off the advances of a girl I wasn't really interested in. I especially didn't want to sit watching the person I was secretly interested in go off with a girl into the woods.

But a group date is a good cover when you've got a secret like mine.

Benjy had been my best friend for as long as I could remember. Before that even. My mom always told me how she'd sit beside Benjy's mom at church when they were both pregnant and how they'd laugh when we both starting kicking at the same time. She said she knew we were destined to be friends after that.

And we were.

My earliest memory of Benjy is of a skinny little kid in a Batman T-shirt who cried when his red crayon broke in half. He was trying to draw Spiderman. It was a good drawing — better than mine — so I handed over my own red crayon. And pushed Robbie Cardinal down for laughing at him for crying. From that moment Benjy and I were best friends. I had his back then and I've had it ever since. I doubt it had ever crossed his mind that anything had changed. He didn't know that his best friend looked at him much differently these days.

Benjy's voice broke into my thoughts.

"You should ask Sadie to the clearing," he

said, kicking a stone ahead of him like it was a soccer ball. He dribbled it from foot to foot. Then he shot his right foot forward, catching the rock on his instep and sending it flying into a tree. He threw his arms up in the air, his T-shirt riding up and showing off a flat, brown stomach. I felt my own stomach flip and looked away quickly.

"Nice shot," I told him. He threw an arm around my neck and pulled me into his side. I could smell the raw scent of him. He smelled of sweat and cologne and hair product and toothpaste and something else I couldn't quite put my finger on. I breathed him in. I wanted to bury my face in his neck. I pulled away and pretended to slam dunk into the nearest tree just to get away from him. Lame. So lame.

"Seriously, man. Sadie's into you. She's wanted you since the third grade," Benjy teased, punching me on the arm. "Dude, she's a sure thing."

"I don't know. I like a challenge," I replied. Yeah, wasn't that the truth.

"Oh come on, Joe. You never hook up with anyone. And Sadie likes you. Just ask her out, man."

Benjy was looking at me expectantly. I shrugged.

"Listen, man, some of the guys are talking."

"What do you mean?" I asked. But I knew exactly what he meant.

Benjy looked away, kicking at another rock. "I don't know. You just never go out with anyone. It's weird."

"It's not weird," I insisted, mildly.

"It kinda is," he muttered, looking at the ground.

I clenched my jaw, thinking about what he was saying. And about the fact that my friends were talking.

"So Sadie, huh?" I asked, not meeting his eyes.

He looked up, smiling. "Yeah, man. She's really into you." He paused. "You should ask her."

I nodded slowly. "Yeah, okay." I swallowed. "She's pretty hot, right?"

"Oh yeah. Definitely. I'm going to see if Brit wants to meet up with me."

"Why Brit?" I asked. "I didn't even know you liked her."

"What's not to like?" He smirked at me. "She's got huge boobs. And I hear she lets you go to second base."

I didn't even know what second base was. But the thought of Benjy getting to it with Brit made me feel a little queasy.

"So what are you waiting for? Call Sadie!" Benjy said.

"I will later," I told him.

"You will not. You'll wait until the last minute, when someone else has asked her. Because you already know that JT likes her and wants to ask her out. Get your phone and call her!" he demanded.

"I will," I promised.

"Now!"

I jumped and grabbed my phone. "Okay, okay. Jeez."

I found Sadie's number and called her. "Hey, Sadie? It's Joe. Littlechief?"

Benjy rolled his eyes. Probably because we had all grown up together and she knew my last name as well as her own.

"Yeah, so anyway . . . I was wondering what you were doing tonight? Nothing? Great. Ummm . . ."

Benjy punched me in the arm and mouthed, "get on with it!"

"Owww! Sorry. I . . . banged my head." Benjy was miming shooting himself. In the head, coincidentally. "Anyway . . . a bunch of us are hanging out in the clearing tonight. Oh you are? Okay. Well, do you want to maybe hang out with me there? You do? Great! So I'll meet you there? Oww!"

Benjy had punched me again in exactly the same spot.

I rubbed my arm. "I mean, I'll pick you up at eight. Okay. Bye."

"Yes!" Benjy yelled and high-fived me hard.

"My man! You have got yourself a date!"

"Yeah!" I smiled. I tried to show Benjy an excitement I didn't feel. And I wondered how the hell I had gotten myself into this.

Chapter 3

The Big Date

I was nervous as I walked over to Sadie's to pick her up. I checked to see if anyone was around and fanned my armpits, trying desperately to dry the sweat that was threatening to drip down my torso. I knocked on the door and waited for someone to answer.

The door flew open. Sadie's mom stood there, wiping her hands on her apron and smiling widely at me.

"Joe! Come in!" she said. "Have you eaten?

Would you like some fry bread? How about a piece of pie? Coffee?"

"No thank you. I'm good. Already ate," I assured her. "Is Sadie ready?" I was sweating again just thinking about having to go on this date.

"Yeah, she is. SADIE!" she yelled without turning away from me. Which means I got an earful of screaming mother.

I smiled through the pain, wondering if my eardrum had vibrated itself apart. "Thanks," I said, far too loudly. I shook my head, trying to regain hearing on the left.

Sadie walked into the room, holding one of her little brothers by the hand. "Hi Joe," she said. She looked down at her brother. "See? I told you Joe was coming. I'll be home later, okay? I'll come in and give you a kiss after my date."

Her brother — I think it was Martin but I always got them mixed up — nodded solemnly. I smiled at him and he hid behind Sadie's leg.

I had known that kid since he was born and he still hid from me.

I smiled at Sadie. "You look really nice," I told her. And she did. She had layered a couple of tank tops and the outer one was hanging off her shoulder. Her cut-off shorts and loose ponytail looked casual but the silver chain and beaded earrings showed she had made a little effort. It occurred to me that most guys probably wouldn't notice so much about her outfit. Or wish they had such good fashion sense.

She beamed at me and smoothed her top down around her hips. "Thank you," she said, smiling shyly. "So do you. Are you ready to go?"

"Yeah, okay."

I said goodbye to Sadie's mom as I led the way out the door. I felt a sharp pang of guilt at the happiness on both their faces. Like me, Sadie didn't go out much. I had grown up with her. She had pushed me in the mud in kindergarten for pulling her hair. She had taught me how to draw a horse. She had shared her lunch with me when I forgot mine. She had been nothing but nice — aside from the mud puddle incident. I always knew she liked me. But when did she start really liking me? Liking me the same way I liked Benjy. Looking at how happy her mom was and the effort Sadie had made to look nice for our date made me feel like the worst person in the world. I wondered briefly, if I didn't fit in with someone like Sadie, where did I belong?

The clearing was a short walk from Sadie's house. There was a path that led through the woods to the area that the local teenagers had taken over and made their own when my mom and Aunt Ava were young. When we inherited it, we brought lawn chairs, coolers, a radio and a bunch of lanterns. We had a fire pit right in the centre and as long as we didn't cause any trouble, the adults left us pretty much alone. The clearing was already full of kids dancing, talking, laughing, and coupling up. I saw Benjy sitting near the fire with Brit in his lap. My heart twisted.

"Want me to get you a drink?" Sadie asked, slipping her hand into mine. She ran her fingers over my knuckles and looked down at my hand, feeling the scars. "How did you get those?" she asked. "It looks like you've been in a few fights," she said, an admiring look on her face.

She was right, if you could call punching a wall repeatedly a fist fight. I knew how stupid and pointless it was. But it wasn't other people I wanted to hurt. And there was something about the pain in my hands that made me feel better for a little while.

"Umm," I tore my gaze away from Benjy and squeezed Sadie's hand, smiling faintly down at her. "Working on my car."

"Well it looks like it must have really hurt," Sadie said. She rubbed her fingers over several years' worth of wall-punching scars while I wished futilely that it was Benjy's hands stroking mine. I pulled out of her grasp.

"I'd actually love a drink. Thanks, Sadie."

She beamed at me and wandered off toward the nearest cooler. She stopped along the way, hugging friends. She was such a sweet girl. I wished with all my heart that I could care for her as much as she did for me. I also wished that I could be as open and affectionate with my friends as she was.

I looked over at Benjy again. I caught his eye and he smirked at me as he gave Brit a squeeze. I tried to smile back.

Sadie had made her way back to me with two cans of pop. She leaned over and handed me the Coke.

"Thanks," I told her, taking a sip.

She lowered herself into my lap and wrapped her arms around my neck, pushing her breasts against my chest. I swallowed hard. Sadie apparently took that for excitement.

Leaning over and breathing heavily into my ear, she whispered, "Let's go."

She stood and took my hand, leading me away from the glow of firelight and the comforting noise of the other kids. I glanced desperately toward Benjy. He saw me being led away into the darkness outside the firelight and winked.

Chapter 4

Making an Effort

The woods blended into inky darkness as we went deeper into the trees. The sounds of music and laughter faded into the background and I found myself completely alone with Sadie.

She turned to me suddenly, pressing herself against me. She kissed me with far more passion than I expected from someone as sweet as Sadie.

The tree branch digging into my back was a welcome distraction. I tried desperately to return her kiss as she thrust her tongue into my mouth. She didn't even pause in her kiss as she reached down and took my hand, placing it firmly on her breast. I felt a bead of cold sweat inch its way down my side.

I concentrated, hoped, *prayed* for a response from my own body . . . *down below.* Anything. I gave Sadie's breast an experimental squeeze and was rewarded with a gasp as she drove her tongue deeper into my mouth. I tried to feel something. But all I could think was that her tongue was about to go down my throat and I'd probably either gag and throw up on her shoes or choke to death.

I felt Sadie's hands at my waist, trying to undo my jeans. I heard the zzzzip as she pulled my fly down and tried to slide her hand in. A picture of Benjy popped into my head suddenly. I jumped away from her as something in my pants finally responded.

"Sorry! I'm sorry," I stammered. "You . . . you don't need to do that."

Sadie looked absolutely mortified. I could tell she had risked a lot being that forward with me. And I pushed her away. I felt terrible that I had let things go so far. But I couldn't get around the fact that being with Sadie that way felt completely wrong.

"But I want to," she said, not meeting my eyes.

I had two choices. I could let her try to get some reaction out of me. Or I could bow out gracefully and try to spare her feelings. I leaned over and kissed her on the cheek.

"Let's go back to the fire," I said, smiling softly at her.

"What did I do wrong?" she asked, her face crumpling.

"Nothing!" I told her, awkwardly rubbing her back. "I just . . . I thought we could take things slow."

I tried to take her hand but she pulled away and started walking back toward the clearing.

"Sadie," I called out at her back. She didn't

even pause. I sighed and followed her. She walked into the clearing and headed straight to where Benjy and Brit were sitting. She started whispering into Brit's ear. Brit glanced up at me and whispered back.

I sank into a chair on the other side of Benjy. I stared into the fire and tried to ignore them.

I drank beer after beer and then switched to a bottle of booze that Benjy had swiped from his parents. I was getting kind of dizzy and the fire was spinning but I could see Sadie surrounded by a group of girls, all chattering, giggling, and looking over at me. I couldn't tune out the sound of their whispering. I took another swig from the bottle, belching loudly and wiping my mouth.

"Easy!" Benjy said, grabbing the bottle away.

"Hey!" I said, clumsily trying to grab it back.

"Party's winding down," Benjy said, standing up. "Brit already left. My mom will be looking for me."

"Where'r you going?" I slurred. I was trying to stand up too, but I couldn't quite get my feet under me. Benjy reached down and hauled me up. I stumbled into him and he threw an arm around me to steady me.

"Come on. I'll help you," he said, leading me out of the clearing and toward home.

The fresh air did absolutely nothing to sober me up. I was unsteady but Benjy's arm around me was warm and comforting. I stared at his full lips, slightly moist from his constant habit of putting on Chapstick. I breathed him in and felt my groin tighten in response.

We walked on. Benjy talked about Brit. I tried to remain upright and ignore how his hand was brushing my chest, sending the blood rushing downwards. I tripped over a root just as we left the treeline and I would have fallen if

Benjy hadn't tightened his arm around me and steadied me with his other hand.

"Easy," he said. "You okay?" He looked at me, concerned. Having Benjy's arm around me felt natural. Much more natural than it had felt when Sadie put her hands on me. Having Benjy so close was intoxicating and comforting in a way that I knew being with Sadie could never be. It was more of a turn-on simply to have Benjy's arm draped around my shoulder than it was having Sadie trying to unzip my pants.

I shook my head, trying to banish the thoughts creeping into my booze-soaked brain. But I couldn't help but wonder what I'd do if it was Benjy trying to take off my pants. Who was I kidding? Even staggering drunk, I knew exactly what I'd do.

He was leaning in so close and looking at me with such care that I did the stupidest thing I have ever done in my life.

I kissed him.

For one glorious, endless second, it was

perfect. I closed my eyes. I felt his soft lips against mine and his unshaven chin scraping gently against my face. I opened my mouth slightly and poked my tongue gently into his mouth.

Benjy shoved me away. Hard. So hard that I was thrown against a tree and slid down it, landing on my ass.

"What the *hell?*" he gasped. He looked completely shocked. I held up a hand, my mouth opening to try to explain myself. "What the hell are you doing, Joe?" he asked again, wiping his mouth with the back of his hand.

"I just . . . I don't know. Nothing. I'm just drunk," I said, getting to my feet by hanging onto the tree. "I'm sorry." Benjy turned and I reached out without thinking and grabbed his arm. "Please," I begged.

"Get *off!*" Benjy shoved me again and I went down. "I'm not a fag, man." I tried to pull myself up again but Benjy stood over me. "Just stay down," he said, shaking his head.

"Benjy, wait! I didn't mean it!" I called out as he turned and started to walk away. "Benjy!" But he hurried to catch up with a group of kids heading home for the night.

I lay on the ground and watched him leave. I knew in my heart that I *had* meant it. For the first time in my life I knew what all the books and movies were about. I had felt my knees go weak. I had felt the butterflies in my stomach when I kissed him. I pushed the thought away as I heard laughter. I hoped desperately that it wasn't at me and what I had just done.

Chapter 5

What Have I Done?

"Stupid, stupid, STUPID!" I was pacing my room and smacking myself in the head with my fist. "What is wrong with you?"

I had sobered up fairly quickly after Benjy left me lying on the ground at the edge of the forest. I couldn't sleep. I had snuck into the house and managed to get into my room without waking up my mom. The last thing I needed was a lecture from her on the evils of "that devil drink" or to be told that I was just like my father. And that wasn't even including what she might do if she knew what really happened.

What had Benjy told people? Were they all talking about me right now? Calling me a fag, like my best friend had? What had Sadie said? That I couldn't get it up for her? I dropped heavily on my bed. My mom would kill me if she found out, and she would. I put my head in my hands and tried to imagine how I could get myself out of this.

I stood up slowly and moved my dresser away from the wall. The spot behind it was marked with patches of dried blood and spots where the drywall had been chipped or dented. I took a deep breath and punched the wall. It hurt but it also felt good. Manly even. Not at all like someone who wanted to be held down and kissed by his best friend in the woods. I punched the wall again and watched as fresh blood smeared across its surface.

I licked at the cuts and sat back down on my

bed, watching my knuckles slowly turn purple. My life was over. By the time I woke up, the rez gossip mill would be in full swing. Anyone who hadn't heard about that kiss at the clearing would know about it before I could do anything. I wished for the millionth time that I could just go to sleep and wake up someone else. Someone who wasn't in love with a guy.

I walked to the bathroom and ran water over my hand I saw a small trickle of blood circle slowly down the drain. I opened the medicine cabinet to get the disinfectant and saw the package of razor blades. I opened it and took one out, watching the moonlight from the window glint off of the metal. I wondered what it would feel like, biting into the skin of this person I hated being. What it would feel like to just cut, deeply, and watch the blood well up and drip down onto the floor.

I held the blade against my wrist and took a deep breath, pressing it so my skin puckered inward. I held my breath and cut, drawing the blade across just enough to draw blood. I watched ruby red droplets bead up along the line I had just drawn and let my breath out with a big whoosh. I deserved this. I deserved to be cut and torn open for what I had done and for who I was. I made another cut, a little deeper this time and felt the blood dripping down my arm. I watched it splatter onto my jeans.

I looked at the dark dots of blood near my zipper. I wished that the razor could cut away the parts of me that I hated. If only I could cut deeply enough to slice away my shame and wake up tomorrow like everyone else. But I couldn't do it. Much as I hated who I was right now, I imagined my mother finding me the next morning, dead and mutilated. Shamed. And I couldn't do that to her.

I slept. A bit. Fitfully. And despite my problems, the sun still rose and cast its warm glow into my room through the open window across from my bed.

I sat up, running a hand through my hair and feeling the fresh bruises on my knuckles. I looked at the scabs already forming on the thin cuts on my wrist. I stood up, pulled a T-shirt and sweats on over my boxers, and padded out of my room and into the kitchen. My mom was sitting at the kitchen table, sipping a cup of tea and staring out the window.

"Morning," I mumbled. I sat down and pulled the bowl of fruit toward me. I had picked out a banana and peeled it before I noticed that my mother hadn't responded. "Mom?" She didn't look at me. Just took another sip of tea before she spoke, her voice low.

"Is it true?" she asked coldly. I stopped with the banana halfway to my mouth, my blood suddenly turned to ice water in my veins.

"Wh . . . what?" I asked, lowering the banana to the table and feeling the colour drain from my face.

"Is. It. True."

I knew what she meant. And that she already knew the answer. I opened my mouth and closed it again, trying to find the words to explain myself but coming up blank.

"Mom . . ." I began. But I was stopped in my tracks when she stood up and walked over, leaning over so she was looking me dead in the eye.

"Berdache!" she spit out. Before I could react or work out what she had said, she drew her hand back and slapped me across the face. Hard. She burst into tears but before I could try to comfort her, she ran from the room and into her bedroom, slamming shut the door.

I put a hand to my cheek, feeling it burn. I listened to my mother sobbing in her bedroom. Because of me.

It wasn't the first time I had seen that look on her face. It was horror and disgust mingled together into something that turned the love she felt for me into hate. She had looked at me the same way once when I was a kid. She had caught me wrapped in the robin's egg blue shawl from her jingle dance regalia and painting my face with her makeup. I didn't understand what I had done to make her look at me like that. I had just wanted to be as beautiful as she was. But she had looked at me with such disgust — such hatred — that I had burst into tears and run from the room. I remembered how she had come in later and found me still wrapped in her shawl. She had gently wiped the makeup from my face with a cloth. When I asked her why I couldn't wear regalia and makeup and dance jingle dance like her, she told me that was only for girls. She must have seen how much it meant to me, because she told me she would make me a beautiful regalia the same colour as hers so I could dance fancy dance with the other boys.

I had seen the fear in her eyes then but I didn't understand it. I saw it again before she started crying in the kitchen. I really wished that I could tell her that she had nothing to worry about. The problem was that, as far as she was concerned, she had everything to worry about.

Chapter 6

Berdache

"I will *never* accept what he is!"

"How can you say that? He's your son!"

"No son of mine would ever choose to be a berdache!"

I winced at the word. Whatever it was, it was obviously not a compliment. I sat on the swing and idly pushed it back and forth with one toe. My mother had called my aunt from her bedroom and Aunt Ava had come over, telling me to wait outside while they talked.

But they forgot to close the kitchen window
and I could hear every single word.

I rubbed at the welt on my face and felt a
flash of anger at my mother's words. As if I'd
choose to be like this. I pulled out my phone
and googled the word berdache. I wanted to
know what it was my mother was calling me.
I scrolled through the results and stopped
suddenly, my face burning with embarrassment.
Berdache was a term used in the eighteenth
and nineteenth centuries meaning "kept boy."
The term came to include all the condemnation
white Christians had for gay sinners. Is that
really what she thought of me?

I started reading some of the articles about
berdache, trying to ignore my mother's voice
as she told my aunt that I was an abomination.
That I'd go to hell for "sinning in my heart." I
was barely aware of Aunt Ava trying to defend
me to my mother.

I tuned them out while I read article
after article. I kept coming across the term

"two-spirited." What was that? I expanded my search to find out about two-spirited people in Aboriginal cultures. I discovered that different First Nations recognized people with both male and female sides to them, who embraced both sides of themselves. Two-spirited people weren't ashamed of who they were and they weren't told that they were abominations by their families. I was amazed to read that two-spirited people were considered to have great gifts. They were called visionaries. They were medicine men, shamans, and warriors of both sexes. Two-spirited. I liked the way that sounded. It was a strong word. Much better than the names my mother was calling me.

I tuned in again to what was happening in the kitchen as my mom continued on her rant.

"I wish I was dead," I heard her say to my aunt. I looked up, listening, my heart pounding. "I'd rather be dead than have a son who is gay."

And there it was. Gay. Just like that. Out in the open.

The thing was, after reading about the whole two-spirit thing, I wasn't sure anymore that it was that simple. I knew I liked guys. But then I thought of the way I had wanted Benjy to pick me up and touch me all over. I thought of how I wished, not that I could want to be with Sadie, but that I could be like her. That I could be sweet and caring, that I could nurture people like she did with her friends and her little brother. I thought of how happy I had felt when I was little, thinking I could just get dressed up and dance with the girls. Not just with them, but as one of them. Was that my feminine side? My two-spiritedness? I put my phone down. Somehow I doubted that my mother would be any more accepting of a two-spirited son than of a gay son.

"He's your son!" I heard my aunt say again.

"What will everyone think? What will Father think?" she moaned. I knew from her tone of voice that she wasn't talking about her own father. She was referring to her priest.

"Ava, Joe is too much like his dad. That's the problem. I tried to raise him as best I could, teach him right from wrong. Show him that our community needs strong men as role models and leaders. Not men like his father. Or ours. I wanted him to be better than them. But he's ended up weak, a sinner. Is it my fault? Did I do something wrong? I need to call Father so we can pray about it," my mom said.

I put my head in my hands and tried not to listen.

I was still sitting outside when my aunt came out of the house and sat down on the swing beside me. I felt her eyes on me but I couldn't think of anything to say. So I swung silently beside her and waited for her to speak.

"You heard all of that?" she asked.

I nodded without looking at her.

She sighed. "She'll come around, Joe."

I shrugged. "I don't think so," I muttered.

"I'll talk to her some more," She reached

over and tousled my hair. "You know I love you, no matter what. It's just that I hate being in the middle," she sighed.

I looked over at her, studying her face. I didn't see any sign of disgust or hatred. I didn't see the failure and despair I heard in my mother's voice when she talked about me.

"Why aren't you upset with me?" I asked softly.

Suddenly my aunt was smiling at me. She reached over and put a hand on my shoulder. "Joe, I've known you were special since you were six. It was when you told me you were going to be a mom when you grew up."

My eyes flooded with tears.

"Mom said I was going to hell." I couldn't help it, but my voice broke. I took a shaky breath and continued. "She said I was an abomination. She called me a berdache."

My aunt stood up and pulled me up with her, enfolding me in her arms. As she hugged me, I closed my eyes and breathed in the familiar scent of her. Fresh baked bread. Coffee. Soil from her garden.

"Your mom and I were raised by nuns, Joe. For her, God was something she could cling to and put every bit of her energy into. I believe in God a little differently. God doesn't make mistakes, Joe. If you're gay, then that's the way God meant you to be."

I felt a million times better for about a minute. Then the air was shattered by an ear-piercing scream from inside the house.

Chapter 7

All Alone

Aunt Ava ran faster than I had ever seen her move. I was right on her heels. We burst into the house, one right after the other. We ran through the kitchen, through the dining room and into the living room without finding my mom. Then I saw the front door standing wide open.

I grabbed my aunt's arm and pointed. She flew through the open door with me a step behind. Maybe it was half a step because when she stopped dead, I slammed into my aunt's substantial back and fell into the door jamb. I couldn't see past her but I heard her gasp.

"What?" I asked, trying to see past her shoulder. I caught a glimpse of my mother standing in front of the house. What was going on out there?

Aunt Ava fairly flew down the stairs and into the yard. Almost without stopping, she used both hands to grab a large wooden sign. It was clear that someone had hammered the sign into the lush green grass of our lawn. Aunt Ava yanked out the sign with one hearty pull. She turned and smashed it against the ground, over and over, until it was shattered into pieces. But not before I had managed to read what was painted on it in bright red letters that dripped like blood.

God Hates Faggots.

My aunt looked over at me, still holding the handle of the sign. For once, I could tell she was completely speechless. My mother looked at me, her mouth hanging open and her eyes staring and accusing me.

"This is your fault," she said, her voice flat.

I turned without a word and went back into the house and to my bedroom. I closed the door of my room firmly behind me and locked it. I left the lights off and lay down on my bed. Reaching over, I plugged my iPod into the stereo dock and pulled my headphones over my ears. As the music drowned out the voices of my mom and Aunt Ava, I closed my eyes. Cloaked in darkness, I realized suddenly that there wasn't one person that I could talk to. Not my mom or my aunt. Not Benjy or Sadie. For the first time in my life, I felt completely and utterly alone.

It was going to be another sleepless night. I lay on my bed and stared at the ceiling, watching the lights from passing cars play across the stucco. My mother had been asleep for hours. But I couldn't even begin to sleep. My life as I knew it was over.

I picked up my phone. I didn't have even one text from any of my friends. I stared at a photo on screen of me and Benjy mugging for the camera before typing out a tentative text to Benjy. I had to reach out to my best friend, even if he wasn't that any more.

Why did you tell everyone?

I waited. A minute that felt like an hour passed before my phone vibrated with a response.

It wasn't me.

I pecked out a reply.

Who else would have known?

But even as I hit send, it occurred to me that anyone could have seen. People could have been standing behind any number of trees, watching. One of the kids in front of us could have turned around at the very moment that I kissed him. I winced just thinking about it.

How could I have been so stupid? I glanced down as my phone vibrated.

I don't know who saw. But everyone knows.

I wasn't surprised. It's not like you could keep secrets for long on the rez. But I didn't even want to imagine what they were all saying about me now. They were my friends and I wanted to talk to them. I wanted to explain myself. I needed to look Benjy in the eye and tell him I was sorry.

And I had to find out who had told everyone.

I pulled my clothes back on and tiptoed through the house. I grabbed my car keys on my way out the front door.

It was a quick drive across the rez. I knew I'd find everyone in the clearing. I stood at the edge of the firelight and watched them; waiting until they noticed me. It didn't take long.

"Littlechief?" A guy named Jake called out. He was a little older than Benjy and me, and was as close to a bully as our group had. "What are you doing lurking around out there in the dark like a little freak?" I felt everyone's eyes on me and swallowed hard, taking a step toward the fire.

"What is he doing here?" I heard someone ask.

"He tried to attack Benjy. Maybe he wants to try again," a familiar voice called out. It was Sadie.

"I didn't attack anyone," I said. I mean, technically I didn't. Acted stupid and inappropriately, yes. But I didn't attack him.

"I was there, Joe. I saw the whole thing," Sadie said. And she laughed. It was an ugly laugh, almost hard enough to hide the hurt behind it.

So it was Sadie who had seen me make a drunken pass at Benjy and who had run to tell everyone. I definitely deserved something for leading her on. But not that.

"He tried to hit on me too!" my friend Trey called out drunkenly. I was shocked. I had never once even considered coming on to Trey. Frankly he wasn't my type.

"That's not true!" I argued. I glanced over at Benjy but he was pointedly avoiding looking anywhere but into the fire.

"Yeah it is," said Trey. "I always knew you were a fag."

Trey took a step toward me. He wasn't the only one. Before I could step back, I was surrounded by drunk kids who were looking for a fight. And apparently the gay kid was an easy target.

I put my hands up in front of me. "I don't want to fight. I just wanted to talk to Benjy," I said.

I saw Benjy glance at me finally, his face blank.

"Anything you want to say to him, you can say to all of us," Brit called out. Her challenge seemed to fire up everyone even more. The grumbling got louder and the group seemed to double in size.

"Benjy?" I called out to him. Maybe if I just apologized, I could walk away before anything got out of hand. Regardless of what they thought of me, everyone knew I was still a kid from the rez and I could throw a punch with the best of them.

Benjy stood up and walked over until he was standing in front of me. The rest of the kids crowded around us, pushing and shoving for a better vantage point. They had to witness everything that went down.

Benjy looked me right in the eye. He waited for me to say something.

"Look man . . . I'm really sorry," I started. "I was drunk. It was a stupid thing to do. I apologize." I stuck out my hand and waited for him to shake it. I needed to make things okay again.

Benjy looked down at my hand and then back up at my face. Before I could react, he hauled off and punched me.

His fist connected with my chin and I went

down hard. Luckily I could take a hit as well as I threw one. But this attack—it was the last thing I was expecting from my best friend.

Everyone started screaming then.

I shook my head, trying to clear the buzz. I looked up at Benjy, the one person outside of my family I really cared about. He was standing over me, looking down. The rest of the group was clamouring to get their own shots in but Benjy held a hand up.

"He's not worth it," he told them. He looked at me again and before I could move, my best friend since I was a kid spit directly in my face.

I wiped his spit away and watched him turn his back on me. Benjy walked away, followed by every single one of my friends.

Chapter 8

Shame

My jaw throbbed all the way home. I knew
I was lucky to have avoided a much worse
beating. If the entire group had been involved
I wasn't sure I would have been able to walk
away at all. Benjy had done me that one
kindness at least.

My heart sank when I pulled into our
driveway. My mother's car was parked out
front. I couldn't face her too. So I let myself in
through the garage door and snuck down the

hall toward the bathroom. I flipped the light switch and stared at my reflection in the mirror. My lip was split and swollen. Blood coated my chin with a layer of gore that I was grateful my mother hadn't seen.

I ran the tap until it was ice cold and soaked a washcloth underneath the tap. I pressed it to my face with a sigh of relief. I opened the medicine cabinet with my spare hand and pulled out the bottle of painkillers left over from when my mom threw out her back.

As soon as I turned off the faucet, I heard my mother shouting at my aunt. Again. Or still. I tried not to listen. I really did. But her words cut through me deeply.

"I have never been so ashamed in my entire life! Everyone knows what my son is. And I hear he's been throwing himself at boys all over the rez and trying to force himself on them. It's disgusting."

I lowered the seat of the toilet and sat

down, closing my eyes. I could taste the coppery bitterness of blood in my mouth. My mother hated me. She thought I was disgusting. And she was ashamed of me.

And I was so utterly tired of my life.

I took the pills out of the bottle and lined them up on the edge of the sink, one by one. There they were, end to end, a long row of painkillers.

"The only thing that Joe is, is your son and my nephew," I heard my aunt say. "He's family. I don't love him any less because he happens to be gay!"

"Well . . . he's not welcome under my roof."

I picked up a pill and swallowed it, looking at the rest of them lined up perfectly.

"As far as I'm concerned, I don't have a son," my mother continued.

I picked up the next pill, then the next, swallowing each pill until there were none left on the sink. I sank to the floor and waited for the pills to work their magic and take this pain away forever. My aunt's voice broke through my reverie.

"Joe is my nephew. I couldn't care less if he's gay. Frankly, if he wants to have sex with the entire starting line-up for the Toronto Blue Jays, I'll support him. I know why you feel the way you do, Mary . . . I know what you've been through in your life. I know why you didn't come home to live with Dad and me when Joe's dad left. I know that you thought that religion was the only way to protect your son. But don't lose him over this. You'll regret it someday."

My eyes filled with tears at my aunt's words. How she could accept me without question when my own mother wouldn't? It was more than I could understand. I felt pulled in two directions . . . an aunt who accepted me and a mother who wouldn't let me in the door. It was too much.

But it wasn't so much that I couldn't face another day. How could I give up when Aunt

Ava wasn't giving up on me? I raised a shaking
hand and pushed two fingers as far down my
throat as I could.

I turned just in time to throw up what
looked like a million undigested pills into
the toilet. I reached up and flushed, watching
them get washed away. No matter what she
thought of me, I just couldn't let my mom find
me dead. I knew I had a future even if I didn't
know what or where it would be.

I spent the night pacing around my room,
trying to decide what to do. I knew my aunt
was completely sincere. She loved me. If it was
up to Aunt Ava, I could stay with her. But my
mother would turn her back on her sister for
opening her door to me. And my grandfather
would never stand for it. It was his house, his
rules.

I went to my dresser and started pulling

out clothes. Jeans. T-shirts. Socks and underwear. I opened up the cigar box I kept on the top shelf of the closet and took out all of my cash. It was money I had saved over the summer, mowing lawns and doing odd jobs for people on the rez. I packed all of it into a backpack, and then padded down the hall and into the bathroom. I grabbed my toothbrush and opened the medicine cabinet, picking out deodorant, an extra tube of toothpaste, and soap. I started down the hall, to the door but paused in front of my mom's room. She might hate me right now but I couldn't leave her without saying goodbye.

I took the notepad out of the drawer in the kitchen and jotted her a note.

Dear Mom. I know that you probably won't understand why I'm leaving. I know I can't stay here and I know you don't want me to. I'm sorry I disappointed you. I'll call you and let you know I'm okay. I love you. Joe.

I had finally got the beater running a couple of weeks before. I figured it should get me to the city. I knew that a city as big and diverse as Toronto had to be more accepting. If there was anyplace I was going to fit in and find other people like me, it was there. I took my keys off the hook by the door and left the house, locking the door silently behind me.

I took one last long look in the rear-view mirror as I drove down the street.

Chapter 9

Running Away

I drove through the night. I drove until the darkness closed in on me and I was struggling to keep my eyes open. I tried rolling down the windows and blaring the radio but I was falling asleep at the wheel.

As soon as I saw a motel, I pulled off the road. A bug light above the door to the front desk buzzed and sparked electric blue as I got out of the car and walked in. A lone man was in the lobby, reading a paperback and digging his hand into a huge bowl of popcorn. He stuffed the kernels into his mouth as I walked in and wiped his greasy hand on the front of his shirt before standing up.

"Help you?" he asked, chewing and swallowing.

"Yeah. Hi," I replied. "I need a room for the night. I was falling asleep at the wheel!" I overshared out of pure nervousness. I pictured him seeing me as a kid and calling my mom.

The clerk nodded. "Right. You wouldn't be expecting any company, would you?" he asked.

"Company? No. Why?" I looked back at him, perplexed.

"I run a clean business, kid. I don't rent rooms by the hour, if you know what I mean."

Understanding dawned on me and I felt my face burn. "No! No, sir. I just need to get some sleep. By myself."

He studied me for a minute.

"Sure. Just need a major credit card," he finally said me.

"Umm. I don't have a credit card," I admitted.

"I'm sorry, kid. I can't let you have a room without a card." He did look truly sorry, I'd give him that.

"Listen. I'm exhausted. I just want to go to bed, wake up and take a shower, and be on my way. I have money. I can pay cash for the room. I'm not going to trash it or anything. I just want to sleep." I looked him directly in the eye. "Please, sir. I've been driving all day."

I watched him take in my swollen lip and smiled as he nodded.

"Okay. Fine. Cash up front. Don't make me regret this, kid."

"I won't," I promised, taking the key card. "Thank you so much."

The room was basic. Just a bed, a desk and chair, and a TV. But all I really wanted was the bed. I probably needed a shower. But I was exhausted. I wasn't entirely sure I wouldn't fall asleep standing in the shower, fall, and hit my head on the tub. I could see the news report now: *Teen dies in motel bathroom*. I fell onto the bed fully clothed and slept without dreaming.

* * *

I woke up, stretched and wondered for a minute where I was. I looked around groggily and took in the beige curtains and carpet before I remembered. I felt a stab of homesickness and looked at my phone. Nothing from my mother. Nothing from Benjy. Nothing at all. I turned it off and headed for the bathroom.

Half an hour later, I felt much better. I would be in Toronto today and I was ready to find something to eat and hit the road with a large coffee sitting in the console beside me. I left the room thinking I could throw my stuff in the car before returning the key card. I had parked right in front of my room. But I looked around the parking lot and saw only two cars. Neither was mine.

"My car is gone!" I burst into the front office in a panic. "It's not in the lot!"

There was a new clerk in reception. She looked up from her magazine and frowned.

"Yeah, we've been seeing that a lot around here. I'll call the police. You can file a report," she said, reaching for the phone.

"No! Don't call them. It's not worth it for my piece of junk." If she called the police they'd want to see my ID, which had my mom's address on it.

She looked at me, but didn't question my lame reason. Probably because they had rented a room to an underage kid without a credit card. "Do you have someone who can come and get you?" she asked.

"Oh yeah. Definitely. I'll just . . . I'll call my dad. No problem at all," I blurted out desperately.

"You're sure?"

"Yeah. I'll go out and call now. Thanks a lot."

"Okay. Let me know if you need anything."

"Thanks."

I walked out of the lobby acting like I didn't have a care in the world. But there was no way I could call the police. I had my backpack and I still had my money. I just needed a ride to the city.

I looked at the highway in front of the motel and watched the cars whizzing past for a few minutes. I stood up and shouldered my pack, then made my way toward the southbound side. Wouldn't be the first time I stuck my thumb out for a ride.

It was a lot easier to hitch a ride on the highway than it was back home. There were about a million more cars going past. The difference was that I didn't know any of the people driving them.

I got a ride right away from a normal looking guy in a BMW. He kept up a steady stream of conversation. He was nice enough when he was talking about his wife and kids and his job in customer service. It was easy to tune him out for a while. I just muttered a generic response every now and then and looked out the window at the passing scenery.

It wasn't until I heard him saying something about "Indians" that I gave him my full attention.

"I'm sorry?" I asked. I glanced over at my host. He reached over and patted my knee. I was too shocked to pull away from him immediately. But a second later, I leaned toward the door, making his hand slide off. He smiled as if nothing was amiss.

"I was wondering if you were an Indian," the man said. I had already forgotten his name.

"An . . . Indian?" I looked at him, perplexed. "I'm First Nations, if that's what you mean?" For all I knew, he thought I was South Asian.

"See? I knew you were an Indian," the man said. He smiled at me and patted my leg again. I pulled it away more deliberately.

"You have a really exotic look," he went on. "You should be a model or something."

This time he rubbed my arm and gave me a look that set off alarms in my head. Something about the way the tip of his tongue was touching his lip made me feel like his hands were all over my body. I shuddered and he took his hand off my arm.

"Not really my thing," I told him. I looked back out the window. We were in the city now — I had seen the Toronto sign a little while ago — but we weren't downtown yet. I just had to keep the guy's hands off me for a little while longer.

"Oh no? You'd do really well as a model. With those cheekbones, you'd make a fortune."

I smiled tightly but didn't respond. There was no way I was going to give him any encouragement. And if he didn't stop touching me, I was going to jump out of the car while it was still moving. It was making my skin crawl, the way he was looking at me. And all the "Indian" talk was seriously creeping me out. He seemed to think my heritage made me something exotic. Something he wanted to devour.

He kept talking about my looks and the people he knew "in the industry." He repeated he could introduce me to them if I wanted. I kept the half-smile on my face and shrugged. I watched out the window for something familiar. We had driven a straight shot down Highway 11 until it turned into Yonge Street. I knew we had to be getting close to the downtown core. He reached over and put his hand on my thigh just as I saw the Eaton Centre on one side and the Hard Rock Cafe on the other. When he stopped at a red light, I grabbed my backpack from between my feet and threw the door open.

"I'll get out here. Thanks for the ride!" I slammed the door in his shocked face and bolted across the street, throwing my backpack over one shoulder.

Chapter 10

Bright Lights, Big City

I didn't know where to look first. I was well aware that I was staring and probably looked like exactly what I was. A kid from the rez who had never been to the big city. But downtown Toronto was amazing. Huge billboards. Lights everywhere. A little concrete park where people were milling around or buying tickets to shows. A cool old theatre. Every kind of restaurant imaginable. People were performing on all four corners of Yonge and Dundas. One guy was drumming wildly on a bunch of plastic buckets while another guy danced in front of him. A bunch of guys from Peru were playing flutes and guitars. A man standing on a wooden crate and screaming about God was getting some weird looks. I thought it was less for what he was yelling than what he was wearing — sandals and a robe. Although as I watched him grab a girl covered in tattoos with multiple piercings and scream in her face that she was going to hell, I had to rethink that. I saw the familiar Tim Hortons logo and figured I could use something to eat. I had missed breakfast. And lunch.

My stomach growled as I held the door open for an older couple and inhaled the familiar smell of coffee and freshly baked pastries. I lined up, my mouth already watering. I ordered the soup and sandwich combo that came with a coffee and took my food to a table in the corner. It was getting late. I'd have to find a place to stay soon. A girl with a pierced eyebrow and blue hair was cleaning the floor beside me.

"Is there somewhere I could get a room around here?" I asked. She looked up at me as if she was surprised someone was talking to her. Maybe she felt that her plain work uniform acted as a disguise.

But she answered in a friendly voice. "There are a couple of hotels nearby. And a few hostels if you're staying awhile."

I had her write down the names and general areas as I finished eating. Then I thanked her and headed out the door, still sipping my coffee. I loved it here in the city! No one was looking at me sideways. No one cared that I had a thing for my best friend. No one cared where I came from. I was just another face in the crowd.

"Ow!" I said as someone bumped into me hard, splashing coffee on my hand. "Excuse me," I told the man, certain I had somehow caused the collision. He nodded and rushed off without meeting my eyes. I looked for a newspaper stand so I could start looking for a job.

I walked into a store on the corner to get a

paper, reaching for my wallet.

It wasn't there.

I checked my other pocket.

Not there either.

I went through all my pockets and searched my backpack.

My wallet was gone.

I suddenly remembered the man who had bumped into me on the street. I thought about how he had rushed off, trying not to look me in the face. I ran out of the store and looked around wildly, in case he was still lurking around. I looked into the faces of everyone passing but I hadn't really noticed what he looked like.

I was in the middle of a strange city with no friends and no place to go. And my wallet had just been lifted.

* * *

Turns out I had actually heard the advice my mother gave me when I visited an aunt and uncle in Winnipeg last summer. She had told me to always keep some money separate from my wallet. When I was packing to run from the rez, I had taken out fifty dollars and put it in one of the socks I had folded in my backpack. So at least I had something. But it wouldn't be enough to get me a room for the night or even a bus ticket back home.

I went back into the Tim Hortons I had just left. I wasn't sure what I was hoping to accomplish there but it was the last place I had seen a friendly face. The girl, Zoey, according to her nametag, was wiping down tables. She must have seen the utter dismay on my face when she looked up, because she tilted her head and studied me for a second.

"Didn't find a place to stay?" she asked.

"I got robbed," I told her.

She didn't look surprised. "Yeah, I should have warned you not to keep your wallet in your pocket. Happens a lot around here."

I sank down into a chair with a sigh.

"I've only been here for a couple of hours," I muttered.

She nodded. "Yeah. Sorry. That really sucks. What are you doing to do?"

"I don't know," I shook my head. "I guess I'll have to figure something out or head back home."

She sat across from me. "Home was rough?" she asked, fiddling with her eyebrow piercing.

"Yeah, well . . . the rez isn't too kind to gay people." It was the first time I had said it out loud.

Zoey nodded. "Yeah. Small towns can be like that. My brother's gay," she admitted. "He came to Toronto about five years ago. Stayed at a youth centre nearby. They really helped him out. They can give you a room and help you land on your feet. If you want."

"Yeah! Thanks. That would be great," I said.

She nodded and wrote down the name and address. "Tell them Zoey sent you. They're cool there."

I thanked her and headed out the door. I wanted to check the place out before it got too late. And Yonge and Dundas had kind of lost its appeal for me.

Chapter 11

Safe Haven

I found the youth centre easily enough. It was straight down Yonge Street from the coffee shop. There were a bunch of kids hanging around outside and it was cleaner than I expected it to be. The friendly receptionist checked me in and nodded sympathetically when I said I didn't have any ID because my wallet was stolen. I don't know if she believed me or not, but she didn't push. She said she could give me a change of clothes if I wanted to shower. I still had my backpack so I was all set. I just wanted to get settled in and try to figure out what I was going to do next.

She walked me to my room and gave me a locker key for my backpack. A shower sounded pretty good by that time. So I left a change of clothes on my bed and locked up the rest of my stuff before heading off.

The hot water felt good on my shoulders. As I let myself relax at little, I started to wonder if I'd finally caught a break. Maybe the youth centre would be able to help me find a job. Maybe I could start over in Toronto. I smiled thinking about it. This could be a new beginning for me.

I stepped out of the shower. I wrapped a towel around my waist, humming as I gathered up my clothes.

"Hey," a voice called out from behind me. I had thought I was alone in the showers. I turned and saw a group of boys at the exit.

"Hey," I said back, wondering if I should

just walk past them.

"Got any cigarettes?" one of the other boys asked.

"I don't smoke. Sorry," I told him, taking a step forward. They stepped closer together, blocking me from leaving. I looked around but there was no one else in the washroom.

"How about money? You have any money?" the first boy asked.

I shook my head. "Sorry. I got my wallet stolen earlier."

Enough was enough. I stepped forward, intending to just push past them and go back to my room. But as soon as I got close enough, they grabbed me. One of them pushed me back into the wall. My towel dropped from my waist in the process. There I was, naked as the day I was born, my bare butt pressed into the concrete wall. A tall, good-looking blond boy stood so close to me that I could feel his breath on my face and the heat from his body.

He looked like a Calvin Klein model with chiselled cheekbones and the bluest eyes I had ever seen. Not even the scowl on his face could make him less attractive. Here I was, being threatened, but my body had its own agenda. I felt myself respond to him. I had never seen someone so perfect in my life. Not even Benjy. I tried to think of something else, *anything* else. But I couldn't help it. I felt myself start to get hard.

"Dude!" one of the boys shouted. "He's got a hard-on!"

The guy pressing himself against me took a step back. He looked down and disgust washed over his handsome face.

"What the hell? Are you some kind of fag?"

I couldn't even answer. The evidence was right there in front of me.

"Aww what's wrong, Brady? Should we leave you and your new girlfriend alone? So you can get butt-naked too?" The boys were laughing now.

Brady clearly wasn't used to being the butt of the joke. So to speak.

"Hey, I'm no fag," he protested. "And I didn't even touch the guy."

He looked at me, probably trying to decide how he was going to recover from this. And then he hauled off and punched me. Hard. In the stomach.

I doubled over as the air went out of me. Brady elbowed me in the back of the head. I leaned back against the wall and stood up just in time for him to punch me in the face, breaking open my swollen lip. The wall was the only thing holding me up now. Another boy moved forward and punched me in the ribs. As I went down, someone kicked me in the back.

"We don't like fags around here," Brady spit out.

Just then, the bathroom door opened and someone walked in.

"What are you doing?" I heard a voice say.

"Brady, go to my office. I warned you about fighting. All of you, get downstairs now."

Brady turned to me and hissed. "You are so dead. I mean it, faggot. As soon as this guy turns his back, I'll come find you. There won't be anyone to stop me next time."

"Now!" the man yelled. He bent down to help me up and handed me a towel to cover myself.

"I'm fine," I gasped.

"Go to your room. I'll send someone up in a minute. I need to deal with those guys. You okay to get there yourself?" he asked.

I nodded, spitting out a mouthful of blood.

I limped back to my room and started pulling on my clothes. It wasn't until I got to my socks that I realized they were the ones I had put my money in. My fifty dollars, my last bit of cash, was gone.

The youth centre wasn't going to be the beacon of hope I had thought it was. I didn't know if Brady was going to hang around and jump me again. I didn't think I'd make out so well next time. I grabbed my backpack and headed back out onto the street.

Chapter 12

A Proposition

I found myself in downtown Toronto with no money, no food, no friends, and no place to stay. I considered turning my phone back on and calling my mom. The desire to beg her to come and get me was overwhelming. But I couldn't do it. She had made it crystal clear that she didn't want me in her house.

I ended up walking around aimlessly. I got off Yonge Street and wandered the side streets a bit. It wasn't as busy here. The stores were more weather-beaten and seemed to sell a lot of off-brand products or electronics off the back of a truck.

"Excuse me," a man's voice called out. I hadn't noticed the car idling beside me. I leaned down a bit and looked at the guy driving.

"Yeah?" I asked.

"Do you want to make some money?" he asked.

There was no way this was a legit offer. I kept walking. "No thanks," I said firmly. I looked straight ahead as I walked but the car kept pace.

"You sure? I'll give you fifty bucks and you don't even have to do anything."

I stopped. "What do you mean I don't have to do anything?" I asked suspiciously.

"I just want you to let me touch you. You can just sit there. You don't even have to touch me back," he said.

I shook my head. "No thanks," I repeated. I started walking again as the man called out from his car. I ignored him and turned the corner, finding myself at the entrance to a huge park. Allan Gardens according to the sign at the entrance.

There was a landscape of flowerbeds and trees. Paths cut throughout the park and I chose one at random and started walking. A couple walked past, holding hands and smiling happily at each other. A woman jogged toward me with a giggling toddler in a stroller. Everyone seemed so happy!

I thought about the guy who had propositioned me. What was it about me that made him think I'd take money from him? For *that*? Was there something about me that screamed "desperation"? Or maybe "homosexual"? Was I some kind of desperate homosexual who would sell himself to a middle-aged man driving a Prius? I shook my head.

I found an unoccupied spot and sat down with my backpack, leaned against a tree and wished I had a book. Or something to eat. I looked around at some of the other people hanging out nearby. A few kids. An old guy clutching a bottle. A lady with a shopping cart and what looked like a pet rat.

"Hey," I heard a rough voice. "Hey!"

I turned. It was the old man with the bottle. Bourbon from what I could see.

"Yeah?" I asked.

"Where are you from?" he asked.

"Eagle Creek First Nation," I told him.

He smiled a mostly toothless grin. "I have family there! Do you know the Archambault family?"

I smiled. "Yeah! I grew up a few houses down from them."

"What's your family name?" he asked.

"Littlechief," I told him.

"Is Robert your granddad?" he asked, grinning.

"Yes! My mom's dad. I use her name."

He shrugged. "I knew Robert Littlechief a long time ago. Went to school with him."

"The Mohawk Institute?" My grandfather had spent years in that residential school. He came out a raging drunk with a violent temper who liked to hit my grandmother and my mom.

The man nodded.

"Name's John," he told me.

I held out my hand and watched as he transferred his bourbon to his left so he could shake it. "I'm Joe," I said.

"Want a drink, Joe?" he held out the bottle to me.

"No thanks. I don't drink."

He took a swig before settling down beside me.

"I don't have much, but you're welcome to share my dinner with me if you'll tell me the news from back home, Joe."

So I did. I told him about Old Mr. Yazzie's decision to eat healthier and how his wife wouldn't cook for him anymore. I told him how my school's lacrosse team was doing. I told him about my Aunt Ava's garden. I described how my grandfather puttered around in it all day and then sat on the porch with a shotgun to keep the rabbits and deer away from the tomatoes. When I told him about my friends and our bonfires, I missed home so much that it hurt.

John nodded. He patted my arm when I got homesick and shared his own stories about his home, his garden, and how much he missed fry bread.

"You'd think I'd miss venison stew or fresh fish right out of the river more. Nope. Fry bread, hot from the pan and smothered in my wife's strawberry preserves."

I could almost taste it.

Chapter 13

Giving In

So that's how I spent my days. I would hang out downtown, asking people for spare change and filling out job applications at every store and restaurant I could find. Not one of them called me for an interview. It wasn't surprising considering my work experience consisted of mowing lawns, helping tend to the sweat lodge back home, and odd jobs like painting. In the city there were too many applicants and not enough jobs. And the few dollars I got from people on the street didn't buy nearly enough food and certainly didn't allow me a bed or shower.

At night, I found a corner in the park with John. We swapped stories, shared what little food we had, and looked out for each other. He made me miss home, but it made things more bearable to have someone to talk to.

John coughed beside me. I pulled his cardigan more tightly around him.

"Are you okay?" I asked. His cough had been getting worse. John waved me off and took a drink from the bottle of water I held out to him.

"I'm fine. Just a cold. I got you something," he announced, rummaging around in one of his shopping bags.

"For me?" I asked, surprised. John pulled out a navy blue hoodie and handed it to me. It looked nearly new. The word GAP written across the front was barely faded. It had been washed enough that it was soft and it was lined in some kind of fleece that made it look invitingly warm.

"John, you didn't have to do this. You should have bought yourself some soup or some cough syrup," I told him.

He shrugged. "Saw it at the Salvation Army and thought you could use it. Nights are getting colder."

"But . . ." I stammered.

"It's okay, son. I had a couple of bucks and you needed something warmer than that old thing." He gestured toward my old sweatshirt.

"You could probably use a new coat," I said, looking at his threadbare overcoat.

"I've got my bottle to keep me warm," he patted his pocket, winking at me.

"Did you start drinking when you came to the city?" I asked.

John shook his head. "Hell no! Me and the bottle go back a long time, Joe. We used to try to make our own back at Mohawk. It was rotgut stuff but it did the trick. Made you forget where you were for a little while."

I nodded. I was curious about John's time at the Mohawk Institute but I didn't want to ask too many questions. I knew how sensitive survivors could be about it. Like my grandfather who never talked about what happened there. Asking him questions had earned me a slap or two.

I changed the subject. I thanked John again and put the hoodie on, marvelling at how much more bearable it made sleeping outside. I had a new hoodie and I had eaten dinner. I had my new friend, John.

But it wasn't enough.

I didn't want to take sponge baths in the restroom at McDonalds. I didn't want to sleep in a park. I didn't want my only friend to be an old man who drank too much. And I didn't want to be constantly hungry.

I found myself dreaming about food. Not the fast food from the dollar menus or the day-old donuts I was living on. Real food from back

home. Fry bread hot from the oil. Indian tacos.
Venison stew with huge chunks of meat, carrots
and potatoes. My mouth fairly watered for
meals that tasted like home. I ate stale donuts
and hot dogs from street carts until I wanted to
scream for vegetables and fruit.

And I went hungry until I finally said yes
to one of those men who drove by trolling for
young boys.

I said yes and climbed in beside a man who
smelled of cigarettes and cheap aftershave.

I said yes and let him unzip his pants and
reach over to take my hand and place it on him.

I said yes until he finished and handed me
two twenties and a ten. And dropped me off
in front of Tim Hortons where I ran into the
washroom and scrubbed my hands for fifteen
minutes with so much soap that I bled the
dispenser dry.

I wiped angrily at my eyes. Then I took
my fifty dollars and bought steak sandwiches
on fresh rolls smothered in onions and gravy,

thick-cut fries drenched in salt and malt
vinegar, and ice-cold Diet Cokes. I took it all
back to the park with me and shared it with
John.

"Where did you get the money for this?"
he asked through a mouthful of tender beef and
onions. I shrugged, gulping down my drink.
He didn't need to hear what I had done for
the money. John had lived on the streets long
enough to have done the same for a hot meal.

Chapter 14

Looking for Trouble

Going with men for money got easier after the first time. And easier still after the second and third time. I put some weight back on. I made sure John ate and I got him some cough syrup. I was surviving. But not really living. I can honestly say my life changed . . . it began even . . . in yet another man's car on yet another night.

I got into a car and earned my fifty dollars. But this guy was different from most of the men who picked me up. He was nervous, and asked me a few times if I was a cop. He kept telling me he had never done anything like this before. He assured me that he wasn't gay, just curious. I tried to calm him down but it just made him edgier. I tried to get out of the car, but he locked the doors. I turned to find a gun pointed at my face. I had grown up around guns, but no one back home was stupid enough to point one at someone's face. I felt my blood run cold and put my hands up.

"Whoa," I said. "You don't have to do that."

"I'm not gay," he insisted.

"Okay. That's alright. I'll just leave then."

"Why did you go and convince me to pick you up?" he moaned.

"What? I didn't . . . you stopped and asked me to get in . . ." I blustered. Then I realized I was just making things worse and shut my mouth with a snap.

"This is your fault!" he screamed at me. "I have a family! I'm not gay!"

"I know. It's okay. It's my fault completely. Just open the door and I'll leave."

"No! You'll tell my wife!" he said. The gun was waving unsteadily at me.

"I won't. I promise. Just unlock the door and you'll never see me again."

He seemed to think about this. I thought I'd be able to get out without any problems. But then he hauled off and pistol-whipped me so hard on the side of the head that I saw stars dancing around in my line of vision. I felt a trickle of blood make its way down my temple as he unlocked the door. I reached for the handle. But just as I opened the door, he leaned over and hit me again. I fell out onto the sidewalk and the car sped off, tires screaming against the asphalt of the alleyway where we had parked.

I shook my head, trying to clear my vision. But the pain was unbearably bad and I felt like throwing up. He had hit me hard, right in the temple. I dragged myself against a dumpster and closed my eyes.

"Are you okay?" A kind-sounding voice broke through the fog.

I looked up at a beautiful girl standing over me. I remember thinking that her skin was the colour of the coffee I drank with my mom on Saturday mornings.

"Yeah," I groaned. "I think so." I tried to stand up but fell back against the dumpster, clutching my head.

"You might have a concussion," the girl said. "Do you have somewhere to go?"

"I sleep in the park," I admitted to her.

She nodded. "I have a place you can stay tonight," she told me.

"Why are you helping me?" I asked her. "Aren't you afraid I'll rob you or something?"

She laughed. "What would you take? Anyway, it doesn't look like you can do much harm to anyone right now."

She helped me up. "It's just around the corner. Can you make it?" she said.

I nodded, wincing at the pain that shot

through my head as I moved it. I was leaning on her more than I cared to admit. But she was strong and managed to hold me up without too much trouble.

"What's your name?" I asked her.

"Obsidian," she replied.

"I've never heard that name before," I told her.

"I made it up," she smiled. She led me past Ryerson University and down an alley to a boarded-up building. "It's right here." She ducked under some construction horses and unlocked a huge padlock with a key she was wearing on a chain around her neck.

"What is this place?" I asked.

"It's an old theatre. They were going to tear it down to make condos but they ran out of money. So I put a lock on it that looks like the kind the construction company would use and no one bothers me. So far, anyway."

She led me into what looked like an office that still had a sofa and movie posters on the walls. She set me down on the couch and turned a camping lantern on.

"So you made up your own name?" I asked.

"Sure. It's better than the name I was born with. Obsidian suits me. It's dark and mysterious. Just like me."

I laughed and then groaned. Obsidian wet a napkin with a bottle of water she took out of a cooler and wiped the blood off my face. I leaned back and closed my eyes. I hadn't slept on a bed — or sofa — in ages.

"Don't fall asleep!" Obsidian called out sharply.

I dragged my eyes open with difficulty. "Why?" I asked, yawning.

"You could have a concussion. You have to stay awake."

She sat down beside me, nudging me upright and handing me a bottle of water.

"You haven't told me your name," she smiled gently at me.

"Joe," I told her, drinking deeply. "My name is Joe Littlechief."

* * *

Obsidian — Sid, as she told me to call her
— asked me questions to keep me awake.
She was really easy to talk to. Maybe it was
the head injury, but I found myself telling
her things that I hadn't told anyone else. I
told her about my crush on Benjy. I told
her how my friends had turned on me when
they found out I was gay. I talked about my
aunt and how she accepted me, no matter
what. I told her that my mother called me a
disgusting abomination and threw me out of
my home.

I even told her that I was suicidal before I
left and had taken whole bottle of painkillers. I
explained how I had made myself throw them
up before they were digested. She listened and
didn't interrupt. She just nodded or murmured
a response.

I told her that I felt so alone and so angry
that I wasn't like everyone else that sometimes

I punched the wall until my hands bled. Sid reached over and took my hands in hers, running her fingers over the scars on my knuckles.

"You can't hurt yourself like that, Joe," she said kindly. "There are people out there who are more than happy to do that for you."

I nodded. She was right.

Talking to Sid, I realized I was slowly starting to accept who I was. I wasn't okay with it yet but I would be.

"So . . . you're a religious, Indigenous gay boy?" she asked with a wink.

I shrugged. "Yeah, I guess so."

"I've got you beat, Joe. I'm an African-Canadian transgender girl."

I looked at her, completely shocked.

"You didn't guess?" she asked, smiling.

"No. Not at all. I thought you were . . . a girl."

"I *am* a girl. I was just born in the wrong body." She shrugged as if it was no big deal.

"Did you always know?" I asked carefully. "I mean . . . if you were born a boy, how did you know you weren't supposed to be one?"

"I always knew," she told me. "As soon as I was old enough to talk, I told my parents I was a girl and I wanted to wear girls' clothes. There was never a time where I thought I was a boy." She shrugged again. "I just knew. It was some genetic accident or something. Like being colour blind, which I also am. Now *that's* a tragedy because I love fashion but I can never tell for sure if my clothes match."

I laughed, feeling comfortable for the first time since I left home.

"Can I ask you something?" I yawned.

"Sure," Sid smiled.

"If you're transgender . . . do you still have . . . I mean . . . do you have . . . you know?" I looked over at her, gesturing downwards and then quickly continued. "Is that offensive? I'm sorry."

"No, no. It's fine. I'd rather people asked questions than just go ahead and make assumptions about me. So to answer your question, no. I haven't had gender confirmation surgery."

"Will you?" I asked. "Get the surgery?"

"I don't know. Maybe when I'm older. I don't really feel like I need to have surgery. I'm okay the way I am. I know I'm a girl," she smiled.

This girl was amazing. Not only had she rescued me when she could have easily ignored me, but she was so confident! She was totally comfortable in her own skin. I wished desperately that I could be like her.

Chapter 15

Sid's Story

I didn't leave Sid's place the next morning. Or the next. Or the next. My head was fine aside from the headache I had for a couple of days, but Sid went out for a bottle of Advil and that helped. She made me feel at home and comfortable with myself. With her. I actually felt happy holed up with her in the theatre. I found myself wanting her around all the time. I hadn't felt this close to anyone since Benjy. It was confusing as hell.

Sid and I walked the streets, taking food to John in the park. With Sid's blessing, I asked John to come and stay in the theatre with us.

"We'll be a family," she told him, taking his hand in hers. John loved Sid. Who wouldn't? Obsidian Smith radiated life.

"I'm happy in my own little corner of the park," he told her, patting her hand.

No matter how much we begged, John wouldn't come back to the theatre with us for more than a visit.

"Why do you think John keeps turning down our invitation to live here?" she asked me later. "You think he's worried he'll catch us fooling around or something?" She wiggled her eyebrows at me teasingly.

"What? No! Of course not!" I was blushing wildly. Which made no sense. Sid was a girl! I glanced over at her, and looking at her face made me blush harder. "It might have something to do with him being sent to residential school," I told her.

"I didn't know he was in one of those schools," she said, looking horrified.

"Yeah. For years. He was in the same school as my grandfather. I thought maybe being locked up in there for so long might be why he prefers not having walls around him." I shrugged. I was guessing. But I knew the school made him an alcoholic. It probably was at least partly why he left his home to live in the park. I knew from seeing my grandfather raging against his past and what the school had done to all those Aboriginal kids.

Sid was nodding slowly. "Yeah. You might be right."

We talked about what we were going to do that night. I wanted to stay in and read one of the books I had picked up from a box left on the sidewalk on Jarvis Street. Sid wanted to hustle enough money to go to the Carlton and see the latest romantic comedy.

I didn't want her going with men unless it was necessary. "Aren't you worried that someone is going to hurt you?" I asked. "That they'll be expecting something . . . that you don't have?" I finished lamely. My face burned but Sid just laughed.

"I just touch them. They don't get to touch me. What they don't know won't hurt them. Or me."

"Oh. Okay then, I guess."

We were draped over velvet chairs in the theatre, passing a bag of grapes back and forth.

"Joe, why did you leave home?" she asked. She peeled the skin off a green grape with her fingers.

"I told you why. My mother didn't want me in her house," I said, choosing a grape from the bag.

"I know. But you said your aunt was okay with your being gay. Couldn't you have stayed with her?"

"No way. Aunt Ava is the younger sister. She might not agree with my mom but she won't go against her. Anyway, she has her hands full with my grandfather. She takes care of him. And my grandfather wouldn't have me in his house once he found out."

"But that's what family is for! If your aunt wanted to be there for you, I can't understand why you'd choose *this* instead," she said, gesturing around us at the theatre.

I shrugged. "She didn't offer, Sid. No one did."

She shook her head. "Joe, if even one of my parents had accepted me, I never would have left. I'd never choose to live here when I could have had a real home," she told me. "Do you know what my parents did when I told them I was transgender and wanted to transition?"

I shook my head.

"My father put me in the hospital. My own father broke my arm and a couple of ribs. He broke my nose and blackened both my eyes and then dumped me in the driveway of the hospital. He left me lying on the concrete in the rain and didn't even honk the horn to let anyone know I was there."

"Oh my God. I'm so sorry, Sid." I was crying now. Not even my mother would be that hateful.

"I had nothing but the clothes on my back. I didn't even have change for the bus. When they let me out of the hospital, I had to walk home. It took me two hours." I reached over and took her hand as she continued. "When I got back to our apartment, I found out that my parents had packed everything up and moved away. They didn't even tell me where. I called my mom's cell phone and she told me that her son was dead and to never call her again."

Sid took a deep, shuddering breath before continuing as I stroked her hand. "Her son. Because it didn't matter to them that I had known I wasn't a boy since I was five years old. They'd rather I was dead than have me become who I was supposed to be."

"What did you do?" I silently cursed her parents for abandoning her.

"I knocked on my neighbour's door. We had known him for years and I thought maybe he'd help me."

"Did he?" I whispered. I was almost afraid to hope that this gentle, beautiful girl had finally caught a break.

"He let me come in and use his shower. He fed me dinner and let me sleep on his couch. And in the middle of the night, he woke me up and told me it was time to pay him back for his generosity."

"No," I breathed.

Sid nodded. "Yeah. I was still recovering from what my father did to me. I couldn't even begin to fight him off with a broken arm and broken ribs. He held me down and raped me, cracking another rib in the process."

"No. Oh, Sid. I'm so sorry," I wished desperately that there was something I could say to make her past disappear. I hugged her tightly. She hugged me back, to make me feel better, I think.

"I got up in the middle of the night and stole his wallet while he was asleep and left. I came to Toronto and never looked back."

I spent the rest of the night, watching Sid while she slept, rubbing her back and covering her up every time she kicked off her blankets. She was right. *She* had reasons to be on the street that I never even imagined. I couldn't begin to understand anyone treating her so horribly. I wished desperately that I had been there to protect her.

I was struggling with how I was feeling about her as I watched her dreaming beside me. I had never had a friend like Sid. I could tell her anything and she'd never judge me or think less of me. What I felt for Sid made me realize that the crush I had on Benjy wasn't really love. I had never been in love. I couldn't help but wonder if that's what this feeling that I was having for Sid was.

But loving Sid brought up a lot of questions about me. Would that mean I wasn't actually gay? Or more gay? I was more confused than I had ever been.

Chapter 16

John's Story

Despite his cough and the colder nights, John still refused to come and stay at the theatre with Sid and me. We had brought him some fresh bread and chicken noodle soup for a picnic dinner. It wasn't fry bread and venison stew but I had walked all the way to Yonge and Bloor for his favourite soup, so he was happy.

John always liked to sit around after dinner and talk late into the night. "All we're missing is the fire," he'd tell me. Tonight was no exception. He ate one last piece of bread, using it to sop up the last of his soup.

He patted his belly. "That hit the spot," he smiled. He lit a hand-rolled cigarette and leaned back in his camp chair. He had downed a few beers with his dinner so he was feeling chatty.

"Did I ever tell you about my home?" he asked.

"No," Sid answered, crossing her legs and settling in for a story.

"I lived in a little mining town right near Joe's home," he gestured toward me. "Up near Sault Ste. Marie." I nodded at him. "When I got out of school, I got a job on a road crew. It was hard work. Manual labour. But it paid well. I met a nice girl and settled down. Never stopped drinking though. My wife hated that. I drank more back then. And I had a temper." He looked ashamed. "We got married. Had a couple of kids. I should have been happy. Bought a little house that we both loved and my wife planted a garden. It was everything

I ever wanted. But I was drinking too much. Drinking up my paycheque. Staying out with the boys. I started showing up at work drunk or hungover. Lost my job."

I was listening intently while Sid held his hand.

"I picked up odd jobs here and there but mostly drank that money away too. I started avoiding going home because my wife would look at me with such sadness in her eyes. So I stayed away. Stayed drunk." He took a breath before continuing. "Went home one night, falling down drunk. She told me to be quiet or I'd wake the kids. I got mad and yelled at her. She cried and told me I had to change, get sober, or she'd leave and take the kids. Told me what a disappointment I was. For the first time in my life, I hit a woman. The only one I had ever loved. Hit her and hit her until I heard the kids crying."

John was crying now, too. Sid was crying. But I wasn't. It sounded so much like my own family. Like so many wasted lives on the rez.

"I ran out and left her bleeding on the floor of our little house. True to her word, she packed up the kids and was gone the next day. Wouldn't take my calls. Wouldn't see me. Wouldn't let me see my kids. Not that I blamed her. But without them, the house wasn't a home anymore. No one would hire a drunk who beat his wife half to death. I packed a few things and I left. I couldn't stay there anymore. Every time I walked into the kitchen I'd see the spot she was lying when I stormed out."

"You've never been back?" Sid asked.

"Nope. Nothing to go back for anymore. My folks are long dead. My wife married a nice guy who treated my kids like his own. And the house has been empty since."

He and Sid kept talking but I couldn't help but think of what had sent me away. Would I stay away forever too? Out of guilt? I took a gulp of water. John was drowning in guilt because of something he did a lifetime ago. I felt guilty because I was gay. For the first time I wondered if I should have stayed on the rez.

❋ ❋ ❋

The next few days were awkward and weird. I didn't know how to act around Sid. I couldn't help but wonder what my growing feelings for her meant. I wasn't sure I was attracted to her. It wasn't about sex, the way it was with Benjy. But I wanted to be around her as much as possible. The only time I really felt good was when I was around her.

But it made things incredibly confusing for me. I stopped wanting to lie together with her, or to sleep or get changed around her. I stopped hugging her like I used to. Soon I found myself avoiding any contact with her.

Sid noticed.

"What *is wrong* with you?" she asked me one afternoon. She had tried to curl up beside me in one of the bigger chairs in the theatre. I had moved away as soon as she sat down.

"Nothing," I answered, not meeting her eyes.

"Seriously, Joe. You're acting really weird lately. Did I do something wrong?" she asked.

"No!" I was horrified "Of course not."

"Then what is it? Every time I come near you, you move away from me. Am I making you uncomfortable?" she asked.

"No! It's not that," I told her.

"Then what?"

I sighed. "I can't tell you."

Sid knelt down in front of me and put her hands on my knees. When I tried to avoid her eyes, she forced me to look at her. "You're my best friend, Joe. You can tell me anything."

Sid had all but saved my life. She had given me a place to stay that felt almost like home. I couldn't keep something from her that was driving a wedge between us.

"Okay. You're right. I'm sorry." I paused. But as soon as I opened my mouth again, the words started pouring out of me. "I've been kind of having feelings for you . . . some kind of feelings. I don't even know what I'm feeling, you know? And I don't know what it even means. Does it mean I'm not gay? Because you're a girl? Or does it still make me gay because you used to be a boy? I just know that I like being around you. I don't worry so much about things when I'm with you. You know? But what does that make me?"

I stopped talking and threw my hands in the air. Sid caught them and held them in hers.

"Joe, it makes you my best friend. You think too much. Not everything needs a label, you know."

I hugged her. Hard.

"I kinda wondered . . ." I began.

"Yes?"

"Well I wondered if maybe I'm not gay. Exactly," I finished lamely.

"What do you mean?" she asked, genuinely interested.

"It's just that . . . I wondered if maybe it's not so cut and dry, you know? I think I'm two-spirited." I pulled up a website on my phone and handed it to her before continuing. "In Aboriginal cultures, two-spirited people are highly valued. They embody both male and female characteristics. And . . . I think that might be me. I mean, it explains a lot I think."

I watched Sid's face as she finished reading. She looked up at me and nodded.

"Yeah," she said. "This is really interesting. And the way Aboriginal people accepted and even celebrated two-spirited people? It's amazing!" She kept scrolling through pages of info and flopped down beside me, pointing out bits of info here and there. And this time, I didn't move away from her.

Chapter 17

Making Plans

I wandered down to the park to visit with John, expecting to see him feeding the pigeons or talking to his favourite squirrel — a grey rodent he called Gregory for some reason. He said it reminded him of a friend he had at school. But John wasn't there. I wandered down toward the conservatory. John loved walking around in there and looking at the flowers and plants. He said it reminded him of home. He wasn't there either. I made my way through the park and was about to head back to the theatre when I spotted him sprawled beside a flowerbed wrapped in a blanket.

I made a beeline for him. I watched as a woman in a navy business suit cut a wide path around him, her face twisted in disgust.

"John!" I called out, dropping to my knees beside him and ignoring the strong smell of alcohol coming off him in waves.

A deep cough tore through him, shaking his whole body.

"Hey Joe." He tried to sit up but he had clearly been drinking all day.

I helped steady him. "Are you okay?" I asked, pushing his hair off his face. I pulled out the elastic holding my own hair back and tied his into a ponytail. "There. That's better."

"Thanks, son," he slurred, patting my arm awkwardly. He coughed again.

"Maybe we should take you to the walk-in clinic," I suggested.

John shook his head violently. "I'm fine," he insisted.

"Did you take the medicine I got for you?" I asked.

He nodded. "Just need to sleep it off," he told me, coughing into his blanket.

"John, maybe you should be sleeping at the theatre with me and Sid."

He shook his head again. "I like it here. I like being able to see the sky." He yawned, leaning his head on my shoulder.

Sid would be wondering where I was. But John started snoring softly, so I leaned back and tried to get comfortable. There was no way I was leaving John alone tonight. I pulled my cell out of my pocket, careful not to wake John and texted Sid.

John needs me. Staying in the park tonight.

Sid and I counted our money every night. We were working on getting bus fare out of the city. I knew I couldn't go back home but I figured Sid and I could find somewhere to live. A city small enough that we could afford to rent a place and big enough that there would be jobs for us. I thought maybe we could head to Peterborough or Belleville. I figured we could rent a basement apartment or something and save up for a real home somewhere.

I told her about the food we made back home, the food I would make for her: venison stew, fry bread, and my Aunt Ava's famous pecan waffles smothered in maple syrup.

"You've got my mouth watering!" Sid laughed. "The only waffles I've ever had came out of a box that says Eggo on it."

"You've never had homemade waffles?"

She shook her head. "Nope. My mother was more of a Kraft Dinner, freezer pizza kind of mother. You know . . . until she ditched me." She raised her eyebrows at me.

"Well, I'd never ditch you. And as soon as we have a little more money, you can taste those waffles for yourself."

"I can't wait. How much more do we need?" she asked.

"Forty-eight dollars more and we have enough take us about one hundred kilometres in any direction we choose."

Sid nodded. "We can make that in one night. One of us just has to get a date and we're ready to start over somewhere else."

"Maybe John can come too," I mused. "I'm worried about him. He's drinking a lot and his cough sounds like it's getting worse."

Sid smiled.

"Of course he's coming with us! It wouldn't be home without John."

* * *

We walked around downtown together that night, knowing it could well be our last night in Toronto. Sid got into it, talking about getting a job in a clothing store. If there was a mall nearby.

"I'd totally rock a job at Hot Topic!" she said confidently.

"You could get me a discount on Pop Funko figures!" I said, smiling.

"Only if you're nice to me," she laughed, sticking out her tongue.

There was a cherry red Audi cruising along beside us. The man inside could have been anyone. Middle-aged and balding with a patchy beard covering his chin. He was staring at Sid with a greasy smile on his face. There was something about him that made my skin crawl.

"What about him?" Sid asked. She nodded over at the guy driving at a snail's pace beside us. The man smiled again and waved at us.

Yeah. There was definitely something creepy about him. "No. He gives me the creeps. We'll find someone else."

"We've been walking around for hours!" Sid complained. "My feet are killing me and I'm hungry. It'll take twenty minutes and we'll have enough money to get bus tickets."

"Not him, Sid. There's something not quite right about him. I can't put my finger on it."

"You're being ridiculous, Joe." She turned to the man and waved back at him. He pulled over and parked beside us. "It'll be fine. He looks nice enough. Even drives a nice car. I can probably get at least seventy-five out of him. Twenty minutes and I'll meet you back here. Okay?" She squeezed my hands and looked at me imploringly. It was that look . . . I could never say no when she gave me that look.

"Fine," I told her. "But right back here in twenty. No longer. I don't trust him." I glanced at him and tried to look threatening.

"You coming?" he called out at Sid, completely ignoring me. Sid hugged me quickly, and then turned.

"You bet, handsome. Nice car." She climbed into the passenger side and winked at me as the man pulled away from the curb.

Chapter 18

Finding Sid

I wandered around, uneasy and checking my phone every few minutes to check the time. The twenty minutes Sid had promised me was taking an eternity. At the ten-minute mark, I wandered back to where Sid had been picked up. I paced back and forth, up and down the street and looked for the red Audi.

At fifteen minutes, I was waiting impatiently for Sid to come back, wishing that she hadn't had to hustle that awful man for money. I shouldn't have let her go with him, I told myself. I should have found a date myself. But the truth was, Sid wasn't one to let anyone tell her what she could or couldn't do. If she wanted to get in the car with that guy, she would. Even if something about him made me incredibly uneasy.

I sighed and looked at my watch. It had been twenty-one minutes since Sid had left with that guy. I looked up and down the street. No sign of her. I walked to the end of the street and looked around the corner. Nothing. I walked back to the other end of the street. No sign of the red Audi. It had now been twenty-seven minutes. Going on half an hour.

Where is Sid?

I called her cell phone. It rang and rang until her chirpy voice rang out.

"Sid! Oh my God . . . where the hell are you?" I said, before realizing that I was talking to her voicemail. I ended the call and looked down the street again. Nothing.

I walked back to the other end of the street and dialled her number again, then stared up in shock as I heard her phone ringing from somewhere nearby. I started walking toward the sound. Then running.

I saw her bag sticking out from behind a dumpster. It was inside an alleyway that neither of us would ever venture into under normal circumstances. But this was far from normal.

I rushed to her bag, hearing her ringtone getting louder. I saw what looked like a broken mannequin stuffed behind the dumpster as I reached down to snag what I knew was purse.

Oh my God. Sid.

"Sid!" I rushed toward her, screaming her name as I fell to the ground beside her. She wasn't moving. I wasn't even sure she was breathing. Her face was a mess of blood and rising bruises. Her nose looked broken and her mouth was so swollen I barely recognized her. I pushed the bloody hair off of her face and tried desperately to see if her chest was rising. There was so much blood! I undid the top buttons of her shirt and saw a stab wound pumping blood. That freak had stabbed her! I was sobbing as I pulled out my phone again and dialled 911.

"Please," I cried to the operator, gently cradling Sid's head in my lap. "My friend has been stabbed. Please help her," I begged.

"Is she breathing?" the operator asked.

"I don't know!" I wailed. I heard my voice, howling like a wild animal.

"Do you know how to check a pulse?" the woman asked, her voice calm.

"Yes." I reached down and placed two fingers on Sid's neck and waited.

I couldn't feel anything.

"I don't feel . . ." Wait! There it was! "I feel it! It's kind of weak, I think. But it's there."

"That's great, sweetheart. Put pressure on the wound. It'll help with the bleeding. Does she have any other injuries?"

"I don't know. She's been beaten up. I think her nose is broken. I can't see if she's been

stabbed anywhere else. She's still unconscious."
Truthfully, I was afraid to look.

"Okay. The ambulance will be there any minute. Just stay with her and keep pressure on the wound."

"I am," I told her.

"You're doing great, sweetheart."

I could hear the sirens now. "I think the ambulance is coming," I told the operator.

"Okay. I'll stay on the line with you until they get there," she assured me.

Within seconds the EMTs were beside me. They took Sid out of my arms and loaded her onto a stretcher.

"What's his name?" one of the EMTs called out to me.

"*Her* name is Obsidian. Sid. Call her Sid." They didn't even bat an eye. I'm sure they'd seen it all by now.

"Sid? Can you hear me?"

There was no response. Quickly they started to load her into the ambulance.

"Can I ride with her?" I asked them desperately.

"Sure. Just stay out the way," one of them told me.

The siren screamed overhead as they worked feverishly on Sid. The ambulance tore across Gerrard toward the hospitals.

"Is she going to be okay?" I asked them.

"We're doing our best," one of them said. I was so panicked, I couldn't understand what it was they were doing to her. They had IVs, electrical leads, syringes, and a bunch of things I couldn't identify. And none of those things were helping enough for them to be sure that Sid would be okay.

As soon as we got to the hospital, the EMTs flew out of the ambulance, pulling Sid's stretcher along with them. As I climbed out awkwardly behind them, I saw several doctors and nurses meet them at the entrance. I followed them through the doors and saw them whisk Sid away. A nurse grabbed my arms as I tried to push my way though the doors.

"You need to wait here, sweetie."

"But she's my best friend," I told her, watching the doors close firmly behind Sid.

"I know. But she's in good hands. She has to go into surgery. I'm going to get you to fill out some forms. Then I'll show you where the surgical waiting room is."

I stood helplessly, looking after Sid as the nurse tried to lead me away toward her desk.

"Will she be okay?" I asked her.

"I hope so, sweetie. I really do. We've got some of the best doctors in the world here. If anyone can help your friend, they can."

I nodded as I let the nurse lead me away, hoping desperately for a miracle for Sid.

Chapter 19

Waiting

I fell heavily into a chair in the waiting room and called John.

"John?" My voice shook with emotion when I heard him say hello. Thank God I had bought him that pay-as-you-go phone for emergencies! I tried to continue but couldn't. All of the fear and horror I felt over seeing Sid after her attack suddenly tied up my tongue. Not knowing how she was doing in surgery — whether she was dead or alive — I couldn't even think about it.

"Joe? Is that you, son?"

I tried to respond — to make a sound. Anything so he'd know I was still there.

"Son? Is everything okay? Are you still there?"

"Yes," I managed to croak out, my throat thick with tears. I swallowed them down and took a deep breath before continuing. "I'm here."

"Are you alright?"

"Yeah. But Sid isn't. I'm at Mount Sinai. They had to take her into surgery and I don't know if she's going to be okay," I managed.

"What! What happened?" he asked anxiously.

"Someone attacked her. They beat her really badly, John." My voice broke again. But somehow I kept breathing and spilled it all out. "She was stabbed. They're trying to help her but they don't know if she's going to make it. Can you come?" Tears dripped down my face as I finished. I couldn't face the possibility of Sid not making it. She had to be okay! She just had to!

"Oh my God. Yes. I'm leaving now. I'll be there soon, Joe."

I hung up feeling slightly better and waited for John.

✹ ✹ ✹

I spent the next couple of hours waiting. Waiting for news of Sid and waiting for John. I paced the waiting room. I counted the tiles on the ceiling. There were forty-eight. I counted the squares of carpet on the floor and then walked down the length of one row and back up the next. I did that covering the waiting room floor once, then turned and went back the other way. Up one row and down the next. Placing one foot in front of the other, other, heel to toe.

When I grew tired of that, I sat down in an armchair and drummed my fingers on my knees. I was sharing the room with a couple of other groups. There was a family who was waiting to hear how the woman's father got through a triple bypass. The other group of tattooed men looked like a motorcycle gang if Sons of Anarchy was any kind of template to go by. I overheard them talking about their friend who had been shot. Apparently it didn't look good.

I called John's cell again and listened as it rang and rang. I was contemplating pacing around the perimeter of the room again when a doctor walked in, pulling his mask down and surveying all of us. My heart felt like it had stopped dead and I felt panic rising in me. He took a deep breath and walked toward me. He wasn't smiling and I found suddenly that I couldn't breathe. He was coming to give me bad news. I could feel it. Just when I felt like I was going to black out, the doctor walked past me and stopped in front of the motorcycle gang. I was right. It was definitely bad news. It just wasn't mine.

I looked away as one of the women with the bikers burst out in loud sobs. I felt terrible for her — for all of them. I wasn't sure if I should say something, like tell them I was sorry for their loss. I lowered myself into a chair just as the door swung open again and another doctor walked in. He surveyed the room and walked purposefully over to me.

I willed my heart to keep beating as I searched his face for some clue. It was completely blank.

"Mr. Littlechief?" he asked, looking down at me from over his reading glasses.

"Yes," I said.

"Is Miss Smith's family here as well?" he asked, glancing around the room.

"She doesn't have any family but me," I told him. "Is she okay, sir?"

"She will be." He smiled and I felt all of the air go out of me suddenly. "She's going to need somewhere to heal. She can't stay on the street. Her stab wound was nearly fatal and it will need to be kept clean and dry. She's got broken ribs and a broken nose, but they will mend. The contusions on her face will heal as well. Your friend is lucky to be alive."

"Thank you so much!" I grabbed his hand and shook it. "I'll take care of her. I promise. Can I see her?" I asked.

"She's in the recovery room at the moment. As soon as she's moved to her own room, someone will come and get you." He smiled at me. "She's lucky you found her when you did, son." He clapped a hand on my shoulder and then turned to go.

"Thank you," I whispered. It was as close to a prayer as I had come in years.

It occurred to me suddenly that John hadn't shown up. I was about to call him again when my phone rang suddenly.

"Hello?" I answered. "John?"

"Hello. This is Officer Walker of the Toronto Police. Who am I speaking to?"

"Umm . . . this is Joe Littlechief."

"Mr. Littlechief, are you a friend of John Burnstick?"

My heart was pounding out of my chest. "Yes, sir. Is John okay?"

"I'm so sorry to have to tell you this, son. Mr. Burnstick passed away."

I dropped back into my chair, trying to remember to breathe.

"What? That's impossible I just talked to him."

"I'm sorry son. Looks like a heart attack. You're the only number in his phone. Does he have any family?"

"Just me," I whispered. Me and Sid. Oh god. How was I going to tell Sid? I listened as the officer gave his condolences and told me where I could pick up John's things. As he hung up I walked to the men's room. I barely made it into a stall before I started sobbing.

Chapter 20

Saving Sid

I had to wait several hours for Sid to be transferred from recovery into a room. I had spent so long in the waiting room that the bikers had long left and the family waiting for news on the triple bypass had received their own good news. I was numb. I was heartbroken about John. But part of me was happy that Sid was going to be okay! I couldn't keep up with the battling feelings in my brain. When a nurse finally came for me, I was dozing with my body sprawled across two chairs.

The walk up to Sid's room seemed endless. I felt like I'd never get there. At the same time, I dreaded seeing what condition she was in. She had come close to death. I was terrified of what I'd find when I walked into her hospital room. And I was terrified she'd ask about John. I stood just outside the doorway and paused.

"It's okay," the nurse smiled. "Go ahead in."

I nodded and squared my shoulders. I pushed open the door and walked in, holding my breath without even being aware I was doing it.

Sid was lying in a hospital bed, looking pale and lost under a stark white sheet. She had a bandage over her nose and her face was marred by bruises. Her hair hung in lanky clumps against her cheeks. *She'd hate that*, I thought to myself. I wished I had a brush so I could at least comb the snarls out for her.

I walked over to the bed and stood over her, watching her chest rise and fall, listening to machines beeping behind her. An IV dripped fluid steadily into her arm through a tube that snaked under the blanket. I sat and took her hand, noticing that her cherry red nail polish was chipped. I made a mental note to bring a hairbrush and some nail polish so I could touch her nails up while she was lying here recovering.

Sid's eyelids fluttered, then opened. I saw her look around the room and panic, until her eyes met mine. She tried to talk, coughed, tried again. When nothing but a squeak came out, I picked up a jug of water and held the straw for her as she drank.

"You probably had a tube down your throat," I told her.

She looked at me questioningly. "Where am I?" she croaked.

I took her hand in mine again. "You're in the hospital," I told her.

"What happened?" she asked.

"You don't remember?" Had she forgotten everything that had happened to her?

"I . . . I'm not sure."

"The guy in the red Audi?" I prodded.

Her eyes opened wide suddenly. "Oh my God," she gasped. Her eyes flooded with tears as she remembered.

"Can you tell me what happened?" I asked her gently, brushing the hair off her face.

"Yeah. I remember some of it," she said. "He was fine at first. Kept complimenting me and telling me how pretty I am." She frowned as the memories returned.

"If you don't want to talk about it . . ." I told her.

"No. No, I do. And you were right about him. I noticed it as soon as he pulled away from the curb. He got impatient. He kept trying to run his hand up my thigh. I pushed it away, tried to turn his focus back on himself. He pulled into the alley and basically dove on top of me. I tried to fight him off but he was too strong. He kept trying to push his hand up my skirt and I scratched his face pretty badly fighting him off. But he pinned me down. As soon as he got his hand up my skirt, he freaked out. Got violent."

I clenched my fists and tried to stop myself from lashing out at something. I glanced at the wall and could almost feel my fist smashing against it. What a relief it would be. I looked back down at Sid and took a deep breath. This wasn't about me.

"I shouldn't have let you go with him," I told her. "I'm sorry."

"You couldn't have stopped me," she admitted. "But there he was, hitting me. I was trying to protect myself. I had my hands over my face but he punched me in the ribs. I heard something crack and put my hands down so he started in on my face. I kept trying to open the car door but he had locked it when I got in. So I was struggling between trying to fend him off and getting out. I finally fell out the door and into the alley. I tried to crawl away . . . it was all I could manage. I thought he'd drive away. But you were right about him. You were."

I shook my head wordlessly. I didn't want to be right. I wished with all my heart that I had been wrong.

"I thought it was over," she continued. "I was actually breathing a sigh of relief that I had gotten off so easy. A couple of broken ribs and some bruises . . . I'd be fine. But instead of hearing him drive off, I heard him open his door. I tried to get up but before I knew it, he was standing over me. I looked up and he punched me dead in the face. I saw stars, Joe. I literally saw stars. I also heard the crunch and knew my nose was broken. Damn him! I always liked my nose."

"Don't worry," I told her. "A plastic surgeon came and looked at it. He said it'll heal perfectly."

"Well that's good to hear!" Sid almost smiled at that. "Would you believe all I could think about was what my face would look like after he beat me up? As if *that* was the thing I should be worried about," she said bitterly.

I felt entirely helpless as I sat rubbing her hand and nodding. Letting her talk. Trying to be there for her and control my rage at the same time. I swallowed my anger, trying to keep my face calm as she continued.

"So I'm lying there on the ground, still thinking he'll finally leave. He had to be finished with me right? Wrong. All of a sudden I felt what I thought was a piece of ice jab into my chest. I obviously knew it wasn't ice. But that's what it felt like. It was so cold going in. And as soon as he pulled it out, I felt like I was on fire. I looked down and saw blood running out of my chest and pooling underneath me. I finally heard his footsteps going back to the car and then heard it pull away. Finally. And Joe? I thought I was going to die. I felt myself just slipping away."

She squeezed my hand back for the first time.

"I thought you were dead when I found you," I admitted.

"I heard your voice," she said, frowning.

"I forgot about it until now. I was gone . . .
floating somewhere else . . . but I heard you."
She smiled at me. "You saved me, Joe."

I didn't have the words to respond to that.
I just squeezed her hand and smiled. Because
the truth was, she probably *would* be dead if I
hadn't found her when I did. And that thought
scared me more than anything I could think of.

Chapter 21

Mourning

I spent two nights beside Sid while she slept. The nurses were nice enough to ignore the posted visiting hours and let me stay. On the third morning, I watched Sid eat and marvelled that she had pulled through. She had been attacked and gone through surgery. I knew she needed as much rest as possible. But first, I needed to do one more thing. Now that she was stronger I had to tell her about John. She had asked about him a couple of times but I had managed to put her off, giving her one vague answer after another.

"Sid," I began. She looked at me so trustingly. How could I tell her what had happened to John? I took a deep breath. "There's something I need to tell you."

"Okay." She smiled a little.

Oh God. I couldn't bear to cause her more pain. But this was something I had to do. Something family would do. "It's about John."

"Is he coming?" She looked toward the door as if to see him walk through it.

"No. He . . ." My voice broke.

Sid frowned slightly. Maybe she could sense what I was about to say.

I swallowed hard and tried again. "John . . . John died."

Sid's eyes filled with tears as I continued.

"He was a lot sicker than he let on I guess. I found out right after your surgery. I had to wait until you were stronger to tell you. I'm so sorry, Sid."

I felt my heart break as Sid sobbed. I held her as she mourned our friend, a man who had been more of a father to us than either of ours. As she cried I thought of all we had lost when John died.

Once she had cried herself to sleep, I got up and went to the nurse's station. I asked to borrow a pair of scissors.

I took the scissors into the men's room. I looked at myself in the mirror and slowly, for John, I cut off my braid.

The police station was pretty close to the hospital. Just a couple blocks down University on Dundas Street. And it wasn't nearly as sketchy as I was expecting it to be. It was actually pretty nice, the glass blocks and windows letting in lots of light. There weren't even any convicts chained to a bench in the lobby.

An officer was sitting behind the desk, typing loudly on his laptop.

"Ummm . . . hi?" I interrupted. He looked up with a scowl. I stepped back from the desk nervously.

"Sorry. Stupid computer keeps freezing on me."

I stepped forward again toward the desk. "Um, did you try rebooting it?"

"Yeah. The tech guys are going to have to deal with it." He closed the computer. "Sorry about that. How can I help you?"

"I got a call to come and get my friend's things. John Burnstick?"

"Which officer called you?"

"Officer Walker."

The cop picked up the phone. "Walker? There's a kid here to see you. Picking up effects." He looked up at me. "What did you say the name was?"

"John Burnstick," I repeated.

"Right. It's Burnstick," he said into the

phone. He hung up. "He'll be right down."

"Thanks." I looked at the posters on the walls while I waited. Mostly STAY IN SCHOOL and DON'T DO DRUGS messages.

"Mr. Littlechief?" A huge guy walked in holding a cardboard box.

"Yes, sir."

He handed the box to me. "I'm very sorry for your loss," he mumbled.

I nodded mutely. Everything that John owned was in my hands. His life had been reduced to the contents of a cardboard box. It made me incredibly sad. I missed him so much at that moment.

I took the box back to the theatre with me. I set it down on the chair John always sat in when he visited. I tried to prepare myself — it really felt like I was invading his privacy. But it was also all I had left of him.

I opened the box carefully. His cardigan was folded neatly on top. I took it out and touched the sleeve gently. There were more clothes underneath and some tattered photos stuffed into an envelope. There were photos of his wife and kids — old photos, nothing recent. There was even one of a young John with them. He looked so happy! They were sitting on the porch of what must be the house he had told us about.

I looked back in the box and saw an envelope addressed to me in John's shaky handwriting. My eyes immediately filled with tears. He had left me a note. I opened it carefully and started reading, hearing John's familiar growl in my head, as if he was right there with me.

Dear Joe,

If you're reading this, then I'm not around anymore and I didn't get a chance to tell you everything I needed to say before this illness finally ran its course. I know I've been sick for a while. But you made the last few months of my life worth it. You and Sid gave me a family again, and for that I am grateful beyond words.

I told you that I left my home behind when my family left. But what I didn't tell you is that I never sold the house. It's still mine, and I'm leaving it to you and Sid. You don't have to stay here anymore. And you don't have to go back to live with people who don't love and respect you just the way you are. You deserve a home. You both do. Go and make my old place a home again.

I'm enclosing the paperwork but I've also filed it with a lawyer. You'll also find my bank information here. I've added your name to the account. All the money I received as compensation from the school and any savings I had is in my safety deposit box. I'm giving you the key and everything in it.

Joe, I chose to run away because I was ashamed. Ashamed of who I was and what I had done to my family. But I'm not that person anymore. I have a family again. You and Sid have taken care of me, and let me redeem myself. And maybe that's your gift, Joe. Maybe that's why you were sent to me and not someone else. Now I want you and Sid to go home and live a good life. I would have been proud to have you for a son, Joe. And I have loved you like a father.

John

There were tears running down my face when I finished reading. They were tears of sadness for John and his self-imposed life on the street and tears of joy for this amazing gift he had given us. A home! I didn't have to go back to my mother's house unless I wanted to. Sid would have a place to heal. We both could have a new life.

Chapter 22

Going Home

Sid was doing well and healing nicely. Her bruises seemed to change colour almost daily. From black, to purple and blue and red, and finally to yellow and green, they were slowly starting to lighten a bit. The ribs would take a while to heal completely. But Sid was up and moving around now. The stab wound was healing nicely. All in all, the doctors considered her a bit of a miracle.

"You should still be flat on your back," one doctor exclaimed when he saw her walking down the hallway with me. One of the nurses happened to be walking past and laughed at that.

"You clearly don't know Sid," she said over her shoulder, throwing a wink our way. Sid had fixed her nails and her hair. She made sure she put a little makeup on whenever she left her room. She actually looked pretty good, all things considered.

And she was eager to get out of the hospital. I had told her about John's letter and that we now had a home to go to. We even had money to rent a car. She bounced between grieving for John and being excited about leaving the city. And she was becoming a pro at a little game we liked to call "when we get home."

"When we get home," she said, being careful not to breathe too deeply, "I'm going to plant a flower garden. NO! A vegetable garden! I'm going to grow the most amazing vegetables, just like John's wife did."

"When we get home, I'm going to find an old beater to replace the one that got stolen. I can fix it up and we can drive anywhere we like," I told her.

"When we get home, I'm going to make spaghetti sauce from scratch with vegetables from my garden. And I'll can it!" she said.

"You know how to can?" I asked her.

"Not yet. But I'm a good cook," she assured me.

"When we get home, I'm going to come out. And I won't care who knows. I'm going to be myself for once. And I'm not going to feel guilty about it anymore," I added, thinking of John.

"Good for you!" Sid cheered. "And when we get home, I'm going to keep being my amazing self."

I laughed. "Hear, hear."

"When we get home I'm only going on dates with people I actually like. People who respect me," she said quietly.

"Me too," I agreed. "Me too."

* * *

It seemed like an eternity until we were finally
on our way in the rental car. Instead of playing
"when we get home," Sid kept up a steady
stream of questions while she sat sprawled with
her bare feet pressing against the windshield.

"So what were you like when you were a
kid?" she asked.

I spent the next twenty minutes or so
prattling on about my childhood. I told her
about my tree house. I made her laugh when I
told her that I insisted on being Catwoman one
Halloween. When my mother refused to buy
me a costume and came home with a Batman
costume instead, I told her how I had cut it
up in my room and sewn it back together into
a Catwoman outfit. My mother was furious
and refused to leave the house with me, but
my aunt proudly took me from house to house

to collect candy. I made the story funny as I told it to Sid, but I remembered how awful my mother had made me feel.

I shifted position as Sid kept throwing out questions.

"How did you do in school?"

"Was there a mall nearby?"

"Do you go to church?"

"Do you have any other family?"

"Are your grandparents still alive?"

"Do you have any hobbies?"

"Do you have pets?"

There really seemed to be no end to the questions that Sid came up with. And I answered every single one with patience and humour.

We left the city behind us. The tall buildings in the rear-view mirror gave way to trees and farms. I sat up and rolled down the window, deeply breathing in the fresh air.

"Smell that?" I interrupted.

"Smell what?" asked Sid, breaking off

a monologue about her childhood pet cat Smokey.

"The fresh air! God, I missed that!"

Sid rolled down her window and stuck her head out like a dog, careful not to hurt her ribs or pull a stitch or anything.

"Are we almost there?" she asked.

"About ten more minutes," I told her. A huge smile lit up Sid's face. She leaned out the window and closed her eyes.

I pulled into the driveway and for the first time on the entire ride home, Sid was silent. She opened the door and stood up, staring at the house, speechless. I walked around and stood beside her.

"Welcome home, Sid," I said, putting an arm around her.

"My family only ever lived in a crappy apartment," she admitted breathlessly.

"I'm your family now," I said. She nodded.

We didn't live in a castle or even a mansion. But it was a nice enough place. And Sid would have her own room right beside mine.

"Do you like it?" I asked her.

"It's perfect," she breathed.

I turned to get our stuff out of the car and heard her whisper, "Thank you, John," under her breath.

Epilogue

The road leading into the rez was as familiar to me as my own reflection in the mirror. I hadn't been back since the night I ran away.

A lot had changed since then. I was living my own authentic life now, as they say. Sid had settled into our new life effortlessly. She had planted her garden and she and our next-door neighbour were elbow deep in tomatoes as I left. They promised to have a lasagna fresh out of the oven waiting for me when I got home. They

had promised me apple pie too. It was enough
to look forward to, so I drove onto the rez with
a smile on my face. People had accepted us. As
long as we didn't cause any trouble they really
didn't care if I was gay. Sid kept busy doing hair
for the ladies in our community and always had
the latest gossip. She was thriving.

And me? Who was I now that I had a real
home and a real family? I was exactly who my
mother had hoped I'd be. I had helped John heal
from a lifetime of pain and I'd saved Sid's life.
If that wasn't being a leader and a role model,
I don't know what was. And I had decided my
path was going to lead me to help other kids like
me and Sid. I had started looking into taking
night courses and I was volunteering at a youth
centre. I thought, maybe, if my mom gave me a
chance, she might actually be proud of me.

I parked my car and got out, walking
toward the door without a hint of shame or
embarrassment. This was me. Take it or leave it.
I might not be welcomed. I might not even be

let in the door. But this was my way of saying that I forgave my mother. If she wanted to get to know me again, I was open to it.

I stood before the door and stopped. I looked around. Everything looked the same. Mrs. Archambault across the road was watering her roses. I waved at her, not really expecting much of a response. She waved back at me. Her roses were doing well this year.

Mrs. Running Bear next door was making fry bread. It reminded me I had to make some for Sid so she could try it. The smell of it made my mouth water. I might have changed while I was away, but the rez sure hadn't.

I knocked, waiting as I heard footsteps inside. The door swung open.

"Hi Mom," I said, smiling at her.

If you or someone you know needs to talk or is looking for more information, there are some great places you can call or visit online. Here are just a few:

PFLAG Canada offers 24/7 support, education and resources for gay, lesbian, bisexual, transgender and questioning people and their friends and families.
1-888-530-6777
www.pflagcanada.ca

Kids Help Phone also has 24/7 counselling and support available for anyone up to age 20 dealing with bullying, abuse, dating, family issues, LGBTQ and more. Live chat via computer or smartphone is also available.
1-800-668-6868
www.kidshelpphone.ca

Trans Lifeline is for transgender people in crisis and anyone struggling with their gender identity.
1-877-330-6366 in Canada
1-877-565-8860 in the USA
www.translifeline.org

Don't be afraid to reach out and get help or ask questions. It really does get better.